She and Alex McMullin were alone in a very small bedroom

"Alex!" Gillian gasped, taking in the reality of the man in a split second, starting with the wavy, jet-black hair and the piercing blue eyes. "You…. What in Sam Hill do you think you're doing—lying in wait for me?"

He laughed. "I'm giving you an illustration of the dangers you're going to be facing—if you let your lieutenant talk you into this job."

"You'll have to excuse me. I'm late for a training session."

When she tried to brush past him, he put a restraining hand on her shoulder. "Yeah. It's already started. I'm your trainer for the afternoon. We're going to be working together, so we might as well get comfortable with each other."

Both of them knew there was no way for them to be comfortable with each other. Not with pictures flashing in her mind of the hot and steamy sex they'd enjoyed before he'd ended the relationship. Was he thinking about that, too?

"I thought I was going over self-defense strategies," she blurted. "This isn't supposed to be anything sexual."

He turned to face her. "You are playing the part of a prostitute. So, by its very nature, your assignment has sexual implications. Depending on how things shake out, you and I could easily end up in bed together."

Dear Harlequin Intrigue Reader,

Temperatures are rising this month at Harlequin Intrigue! So whether our mesmerizing men of action are steaming up their love lives or packing heat in high-stakes situations, July's lineup is guaranteed to sizzle!

Back by popular demand is the newest branch of our Confidential series. Meet the heroes of NEW ORLEANS CONFIDENTIAL—tough undercover operatives who will stop at nothing to rid the streets of a crime ring tied to the most dangerous movers and shakers in town. *USA TODAY* bestselling author Rebecca York launches the series with *Undercover Encounter*—a darkly sensual tale about a secret agent who uses every resource at his disposal to get his former flame out alive when she goes deep undercover in the sultry French Quarter.

The highly acclaimed Gayle Wilson returns to the lineup with *Sight Unseen*. In book three of PHOENIX BROTHERHOOD, it's a race against time to prevent a powerful terrorist organization from unleashing unspeakable harm. Prepare to become entangled in *Velvet Ropes* by Patricia Rosemoor—book three in CLUB UNDERCOVER—when a clandestine investigation plunges a couple into danger….

Our sassy inline continuity SHOTGUN SALLYS ends with a bang! You won't want to miss *Lawful Engagement* by Linda O. Johnston. In Cassie Miles's newest Harlequin Intrigue title—*Protecting the Innocent*—a widow trapped in a labyrinth of evil brings out the Achilles' heel in a duplicitous man of mystery.

Delores Fossen's newest thriller is not to be missed. *Veiled Intentions* arouses searing desires when two bickering cops pose as doting fiancés in their pursuit of a deranged sniper!

Enjoy our explosive lineup this month!

Denise O'Sullivan
Senior Editor, Harlequin Intrigue

UNDERCOVER ENCOUNTER

USA TODAY Bestselling Author

REBECCA YORK

RUTH GLICK WRITING AS REBECCA YORK

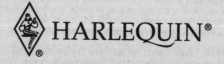

TORONTO • NEW YORK • LONDON
AMSTERDAM • PARIS • SYDNEY • HAMBURG
STOCKHOLM • ATHENS • TOKYO • MILAN • MADRID
PRAGUE • WARSAW • BUDAPEST • AUCKLAND

Special thanks and acknowledgment are given to Rebecca York for her contribution to the NEW ORLEANS CONFIDENTIAL series.

ISBN 0-373-22783-3

UNDERCOVER ENCOUNTER

ABOUT THE AUTHOR

Award-winning, bestselling novelist Ruth Glick, who writes as Rebecca York, is the author of close to eighty books, including her popular 43 LIGHT STREET series for Harlequin Intrigue. Ruth says she has the best job in the world. Not only does she get paid for telling stories, she's also the author of twelve cookbooks. Ruth and her husband, Norman, travel frequently, researching locales for her novels and searching out new dishes for her cookbooks.

Books by Rebecca York

THE CONFIDENTIAL AGENT'S PLEDGE

I hereby swear to uphold the law
to the best of my ability; to maintain the level of
integrity of this agency by my compassion for victims,
loyalty to my brothers and courage under fire.

And above all, to hold all information and identities
in the strictest confidence...

CAST OF CHARACTERS

Alexander McMullin—He was a tough cop who quit the NOPD. Now he's working for New Orleans Confidential on a top-secret case.

Gillian Seymour—A rookie cop, she takes a dangerous undercover assignment to clean up the streets of the Big Easy and forms an uneasy alliance with the man from her past.

Wiley Longbottom—The retired director of Colorado Department of Public Safety came to New Orleans to have a good time and ended up close to death.

Conrad Burke—As head of NOC, he's determined to find out who put Wiley Longbottom in the hospital.

Seth Lewis—A rough-around-the-edges Confidential operative.

Tanner Harrison—This world-weary ex-CIA agent has problems he doesn't even know about....

Maurice Gaspard—The pimp who cracks the whip at the elegant bordello called the McDonough Club.

Madame Cynthia Dupré—She keeps the working girls in line and the customers satisfied at the McDonough Club.

Jack Smith—This bartender mixes drugs with drinks at Bourbon Street Libations.

Lily—This frightened teenage runaway is "working" at the McDonough Club, but she didn't volunteer for the job.

Ricardo Gonzalez—Evil to the core, he plans to overthrow the government of Nilia, a South American country.

Jerome Senegal—This ruthless and wealthy New Orleans businessman is in over his head with Gonzalez.

Sebastion Primeaux—Both powerful and corrupt, this district attorney knows how to keep the right people happy.

Prologue

"It's not your fault," Alexander McMullin said from the doorway of the hospital room.

Conrad Burke, who was standing by the window with his head bowed, looked up, his countenance a mixture of determination and anger. He was tall, with dark hair and dark eyes—in the prime of his life. A stark contrast to the other occupant of the room who lay in the narrow bed, his eyes closed, his breathing shallow.

The unconscious man had once been slightly rotund. Now his body seemed to have shrunken and his thinning dark hair was plastered to his head.

As Alex stepped across the threshold, Conrad turned to face him squarely, the way he always faced what life threw at him. Yet he couldn't hide the haunted look in his eyes.

Until a few months ago Conrad had been with the Colorado Confidential operation, run out of the Royal Flush Ranch by Colleen Wellesley. Then he'd been tapped to set up New Orleans Confidential, so he'd moved his wife and twin babies to the city.

One of the first agents recruited for the new branch, Alex was determined to keep Conrad from doing something he'd regret.

His new boss gave him a direct look. "What do you

mean, this isn't my fault?'' Conrad gestured toward the unconscious man. ''I'm the one who invited Wiley down to New Orleans. I'm the one who took him out for a night on the town. If I'd just left well enough alone, he'd be fine now.''

Keeping his voice even, Alex said, ''You didn't slip him the drug that put him in that hospital bed. Nobody could have anticipated that would happen.''

Conrad's expression only became more self-accusatory. ''I'm supposed to know what's going on in this city.''

''You just moved back here. New Orleans Confidential isn't even operational yet.''

The other man ignored him and plowed on. ''Why the hell did I have to take him to Bourbon Street Libations, of all places?''

''Because you didn't know the bartender was drugging the customers.''

It had all started so innocently, Alex thought. Wiley Longbottom, the man who lay in this hospital bed close to death, was the former director of the Colorado Department of Public Safety, aka Colorado Confidential. A heart condition had forced him into early retirement.

And Conrad Burke, who'd worked with Wiley at the secret government agency, had invited his old boss down to the Crescent City for a big, blowout going-away party.

The first few hours had been a blast—with the new agents like Alex listening to the old hands play ''can you top this'' as they exchanged stories about shoot-outs and undercover operations. Wiley and Philip Jones, one of the Confidential recruits who'd worked as a P.I. in the city for years, had everyone else convulsing with laughter at their escapades.

Unfortunately, the evening hadn't turned out the way anyone expected—because good old Jack Smith, who

tended bar at Bourbon Street Libations, had slipped something into the retired director's drink.

Something very nasty and very potent. And not just one
dose of the stuff. It was a drug they were now calling Category Five because it swept through the unsuspecting vic-
tim like a major hurricane. It had made straight-arrow Wiley horny as hell. When one of the prostitutes who
frequented the bar came on to him, he leaped at the chance
to leave with her. Everyone at the table thought he'd wake
up in the morning with a hell of a hangover and an embarrassed grin on his face—until they checked his hotel
room and found that he'd never come home that night.

After a frantic search, they'd found him in the intensive
care unit of St. Charles General Hospital, suffering from a
massive heart attack.

Conrad's voice interrupted Alex's dark thoughts. "We're
going to get the bastards that did this to Wiley. We're going
operational next week."

Alex had expected something like that, although he knew
they weren't nearly ready. They'd just gotten their undercover operation—a trucking company called Crescent City
Transports—in halfway working order.

"How do we justify jumping in two months early? I
mean, what's the official explanation?"

"I'll come up with something."

Privately, Alex didn't like the setup. But he understood
where Conrad was coming from. So all he said was, "Tell
me what you need from me."

Chapter One

"Hey, buddy, hurry up with that damn beer," a sharp voice cut through the babble of voices and music blaring through Bourbon Street Libations.

"Coming right up," Alex McMullin answered as he pulled back on the tap and filled a glass, then delivered the brew to an impatient tourist. Next, he wiped up a spill on the polished bar and pocketed a generous tip from a customer. Working undercover as a bartender had its advantages, although he sure hadn't thought he'd end up dispensing booze when he'd joined New Orleans Confidential.

But this was the bar, Bourbon Street Libations, where Wiley Longbottom had been drugged. Which was why Alex was presently making a Singapore Sling for another boozy tourist—while keeping the small, wiry figure of the other bartender, Jack Smith, in his peripheral vision.

A noise coming from the direction of the door made Alex's head jerk up. A big, muscular guy named Tony was supposed to be at the entrance, politely turning away anyone who was too plastered to whistle "Dixie." But he'd gone on his break a few minutes ago, leaving the belligerent drunk who'd just staggered into the bar free to take a swing at another patron.

Alex looked at Jack, who shrugged and bent his balding

head toward the drink he was mixing. Alex also glanced at Mason Bartley, the most unlikely member of the Confidential team, a forty-year-old loser with short brown hair and shifty blue eyes. At the moment he was acting true to form, looking down into his rum and Coke.

With no one else prepared to keep order, Alex rounded the bar and headed for the drunk, who immediately tried to pop him one.

"No, you don't," he growled. Spinning the guy around, he propelled him toward the door.

Instead of going quietly, the guy made a furtive motion toward his boot, and a knife that could gut a pig materialized in his hand. Only, he wasn't after pork this evening. With a curse, he made a vicious slash at Alex's midsection.

Acting instinctively, Alex aimed a kick at the guy's arm, sending him sprawling on the barroom floor and the knife flying.

The jerk was stupid enough to lunge for the weapon again. Alex kicked it out of the way, wondering if he was going to have to do some serious damage.

Someone in the back must have alerted Tony because he came rushing into the fray and scooped up the pork sticker. Of course, by this time, the little altercation was attracting a crowd, from both inside and outside the bar. Tony must have figured Alex could take care of the intruder, because he turned his own attention to settling down the rest of the patrons.

As a former police detective, Alex's instinct was to call the boys in blue and let them haul this guy's ass away. But Bourbon Street Libations had a pretty strict no-cops policy. Unless somebody got killed, you kept the law out of it.

So he frog-marched the drunk onto the street where they were instantly enveloped by the heat and humidity of the night.

"Need some help?" a voice from the crowd asked. Alex looked up to see Rich Stewart—dressed in a nicely authentic biker outfit—ambling toward him. A former navy SEAL who still kept his dark blond hair in a short military cut, he was another of the Confidential agents. With a grin, he helped Alex propel the inebriated jerk several paces down the block.

When Alex turned, he saw Tony stepping onto the street. "Thanks," he muttered. "Sorry, I was in the can when the excitement broke loose."

"No problem," Alex answered. Actually he'd been enjoying the action. Standing behind a bar didn't give him much opportunity for aerobic activity—unless you counted wielding a cocktail shaker.

Now that he was away from his post, he allowed himself a few minutes of relaxation. Dragging in a breath of the humid air, he watch the boisterous crowd parading up and down the most famous street in the French Quarter, past bars, strip joints, boutiques selling cheap souvenirs and voodoo hexes, and, of course, the all-essential condom shop up the way.

Music blared from the bars and jazz clubs, mingling with the raunchy conversation of the crowd. Bourbon Street at night was a party animal's playground. Or a trap for the unwary.

The doctor had told Conrad that the hospital had seen several older men come in under circumstances similar to Wiley Longbottom's. They'd all ingested an unidentified drug that stimulated the libido but had the dangerous side effect of elevating the heart rate to the extreme. Demanding answers, Conrad had contacted Police Chief Henri Courville, who'd immediately gone into defensive mode, claiming that his department was putting all the resources it could spare into tracking the source of the new designer drug.

After some initial finger-pointing, Conrad and the police chief had calmed down enough to play ball with each other. Which was why New Orleans Confidential was now running a joint operation with the P.D.

The arrangement didn't exactly thrill Alex.

His last couple of years as a police detective had been marred by red tape and departmental screwups. The final straw had come after he'd busted his butt to get the evidence for a capital murder case—and the conviction had been thrown out due to a legal loophole.

After that, the job simply hadn't been the same. He'd taken a leave of absence from the force, done some freelance investigative work and spent a lot of time fixing up the house he'd bought, wondering if he could support himself as a private eye. Then Conrad Burke had tracked him down and made him an offer, and he'd jumped at the chance to work for a man he respected.

Unfortunately now he was stuck having to make both Conrad Burke and Henri Courville happy.

Down the street, a man was leaning over one of the wrought-iron balconies and tossing newly minted faux "doubloons" and cheap necklaces to a rowdy crowd. Once such activity had been strictly a feature of Mardi Gras. Now you saw it all the time down here. He eyed some of the girls down below, wondering if one of them would take off her T-shirt and bra to get some loot thrown her way. When all the ladies kept their shirts on, he went back into the bar.

Jack gave him a narrow-eyed look. "Nice of you to join us. We're pretty busy in here."

Alex shrugged. He and Jack had a pretty prickly relationship. "The next time we get a guy with a knife, you can take care of him."

"Not my job."

Alex didn't bother to answer. He already knew that Jack was pretty busy—mixing drinks and pushing drugs. A dangerous combination. It was only a matter of time before the little squirt got himself into serious trouble.

They stayed out of each other's way for the next half hour. Then a group of five overdressed older businessmen, looking like they were out slumming, came into the bar and took a table on the right. After the scantily clad cocktail waitress wrote down their drink requests, she headed for Alex. But Jack signaled her to come to him instead.

"I owe you one," he said to Alex as he scanned the order, then began making Hurricanes. Alex gave him a thumbs-up and went back to work on a batch of Margaritas for some wet-behind-the-ears college kids. But he kept tabs on Jack. The guy bent down below the level of the bar. When he came back up, it looked like the cuff of his long-sleeved shirt was bulging just a little. As he mixed one of the Hurricanes, a fine mist of white powder fell from underneath the cuff into the drink. Not powdered sugar, Alex thought as he watched the bartender stir the stuff into the drink.

He'd bet his nonexistent New Orleans P.D. pension that it was Category Five.

The prime targets for this deadly designer drug were older affluent men. It aroused them sexually—allowing prostitutes to prey on them—but if too much was contained they could die of heart attacks. The cop in him wanted to warn the businessmen. But, since Wiley's heart attack, nobody else had ended up in the hospital. And giving out warnings would jeopardize the joint undercover NOC-PD operation.

So he watched the waitress swish her hips over to the table and chat with the guys while she distributed the drinks. He kept an eye on the men, seeing the symptoms develop in one of them, the same signs he'd seen in Wiley. The guy with the spiked drink got red in the face, shifted in his seat and began talking pretty loudly.

Obviously embarrassed, the others in his group tried to calm him down, but he wasn't willing to be restrained. Over the next twenty minutes, he became increasingly obnoxious.

When a little working girl at a nearby table caught his eye, he left his friends and went over to sit with her. Probably they were glad to get rid of him.

Mentally taking notes, Alex watched the guy indiscreetly paw at her in public before they headed for the front door.

Alex wanted to find out where they were going. Since the crowd in the bar had thinned, he tossed an "I'll be right back" in Jack's direction.

Before the other bartender could object, he hurried down the hall toward the men's room, then made for the back exit where he ducked into the alley, gagging at the smell of garbage bags waiting to be picked up in the morning. The couple had gone out the front door. He charged down the alley and through a passageway that led from a private garden back to the street. There he scanned the crowd. But his quarry had disappeared. He couldn't take a chance on passing Tony at the door. His only option was to search in the opposite direction—toward the far end of Bourbon Street where the lights were lower and the crowds were thinner.

He thought he'd lost the pair. But his luck held and he caught a glimpse of the happy couple just turning the corner.

Probably the guy wouldn't realize he was being followed. But the woman might catch on. Playing safe, Alex hung back, watching them make for a sprawling stucco building with Ionic columns holding up a small portico in front. When they disappeared inside, he hugged the shadows across the street and strolled past, looking at the name above the door. The McDonough Club.

He blinked, thinking he'd read it wrong. But the words stayed the same.

He'd heard of the place. It was an old and distinguished men's club, named after one of the city's benefactors. Could the working girl really be planning to take her date here?

Well, they'd gone inside. He'd report that at the morning meeting and check out the vital statistics on the club.

Meanwhile he'd better get back before he lost his job.

By sprinting all the way, he arrived at the alley door of the bar about ten minutes after he'd left. Ducking into the men's room, he took a couple of deep breaths and washed his hands. When he glanced at his watch he saw that it was half past midnight. In a couple of hours he could go home and catch a little sleep. Then it was on to his other assignment—playing truck driver.

Jack gave him a dirty look when he returned. But he pretended to be oblivious.

He was hoping that the rest of the evening would be less eventful. But no such luck. Twenty minutes later, as he drew another draft of beer, his attention zinged to the front door when three dark Latino men swaggered into the bar. All of them were large and muscular, with slicked-down black hair, new jeans and dark T-shirts. Actually, Alex was surprised when Tony stepped aside and let them in, since they looked like trouble.

They took a table in the back, speaking Spanish and acting as though they owned the place. As he glanced at them from time to time, Alex began making connections. They looked as if they could be some of the Nilia rebels due to arrive in town.

The rebels were the reason the Department of Public Safety had opened this new branch of Confidential in New Orleans in the first place. Their leader, Ricardo Gonzalez, aka "Black Death," was bent on overthrowing the government of a country that reminded Alex a lot of Venezuela. Gonzalez wanted to squelch the peaceful democracy that existed there and grab the considerable oil resources. And he was willing to use any means at his disposal, including wiping out whole villages to make an example of them.

CIA agents who had been in-country following his movements had discovered that a group of Gonzalez's men was headed toward New Orleans.

Alex watched them without being obvious. He'd heard that everyone who worked for Gonzalez had a scorpion tattooed on his upper body. If he tore the shirt off one of them, would he find the mark?

He was pretty sure there wasn't much chance of undressing any of them in here. He saw that Rich Stewart had drifted into the bar and was glad the other agent was keeping tabs on the action, since the newcomers' behavior was definitely something to worry about. Looking up, he saw one of them deliberately bump his chair into that of another patron, apparently for the sheer pleasure of seeing if he could start a fight.

The other guy moved out of the way, and the group went back to their drinks—until one of them made eye contact with a blond coed. When she smiled at him, he made a spontaneous decision that he was going to separate her from her boyfriend.

Clearing a path through the bar, he moved in on the kids, leaning over the girl with his big hand on her shoulder and his fingers coming down over her breast.

Rich and Alex exchanged glances. Rich edged a little closer to the group, but stayed out of their way.

With the noise level in the room, it was impossible for Alex to hear anything that was being said. Still, it was obvious that the college boy was mad as hell—but also afraid to tangle with the hulking Hispanic.

Alex clenched his fist around the spout of the soda and soft drink dispenser, wishing that he could help the kid out. But he'd already called enough attention to himself for one night.

The other members of the macho group sat back, enjoying the fun, laughing among themselves. But just as their amigo was about to chew the kid up and spit him out, the others mercifully stepped in to drag their cohort out of the bar. And Alex breathed out a little sigh. Disaster averted, and he hadn't even stuck his nose into it.

He glanced up, seeing Rich give a small nod before following them into the street. Mason stayed where he was. Over the past few days Alex was getting the impression that his specialty was avoiding trouble.

Alex spent the next half hour tending bar and feeling almost like he was on break.

But his antenna went up when another prostitute walked through the door. She'd picked a slow time, which immediately made him think she was one of the police recruits getting some training when there wouldn't be too much chance of fending off propositions.

She was wearing a lot of makeup, but as she stood inside the door scanning the room, Alex got a good look at her face.

His heart clunked inside his chest, then started up a rapid beat that made it hard to breathe.

The prostitute was Gillian Seymour. He'd know that fiery redhead anywhere, even dressed in a low-cut blouse, a miniskirt that barely covered her crotch, fishnet stockings and little black boots.

While he'd still been with the N.O.P.D., he and Gillian had dated. Well, that was a pretty mild word for the torrid affair that had rocketed to life between them.

Truthfully, she'd been the best thing in his life at the time. But even as the two of them had driven each other to ecstasy in bed, he'd known that he was no good for her. So he'd broken it off.

For a painful second he allowed himself to envy his boss. Conrad Burke was married to a wonderful woman named Marilyn whom he'd met on one of his previous assignments. They were raising a set of twins—a boy and a girl. That was the way life was supposed to be. A man and a woman fell in love, settled down and raised a family.

Unfortunately it hadn't been that way with his own parents. Mom and Dad had each been married five times. Alex was their oldest kid. The one who'd been born while they weren't hitched to anyone. And he couldn't even keep up with all the stepsisters and brothers from the various unions—the shortest of which had lasted four months.

As a kid, he'd been shuffled from one parent to the next and back again—often feeling like he'd gotten lost in the cracks of his parents' new relationships.

And he'd vowed never to do that to a child of his own. He knew he wasn't a suitable candidate for marriage. It just wasn't in his genes. So he'd always kept his dealings with the fair sex superficial.

Which was what had scared him about Gillian. He'd wanted her on a level that he wasn't prepared to accept—which had finally sent him running in the other direction.

But in the two years since breaking off the affair he'd thought of her often. And when he'd heard she'd entered the police academy, he'd wondered if her idealism would last once she started patrolling the city's mean streets.

How long had she been in uniform? She'd have started out as a beat cop. But if she was already doing undercover work, then someone had noticed her potential and put her on the department fast track.

Which was too damn bad. She'd burn out as fast as he had if they kept pushing her into the "choice" assignments. And one thing he knew from the way she clasped her hands together in front of her; she was nervous. Which proved she was too green to be playing the tricky undercover part of a prostitute.

He studied her for half a minute. Lord, that red hair looked like it could set the place on fire. Or burn a man's fingers. And the skimpy outfit displayed the nicely curved figure he remembered very well.

Under the makeup that she'd applied with a trowel, he could see that her features were still striking.

He kept his gaze on her, willing her to look in his direction. He knew the exact moment when she spotted him standing rigidly behind the bar. Her jaw didn't exactly drop open. But she froze, standing near the doorway for a couple of electric seconds, then tilted her chin up and looked deliberately away.

It was all he could do to keep from charging around the bar and demanding to know if she'd lost her mind.

But he stayed where he was, his eyes narrowing as he watched her survey the room, then head for a table where two guys were sitting. Both were wearing short-sleeved, button-down shirts. Both looked like they'd had about three drinks too many. The French Quarter had that effect on civilians, Alex mused. There were too many bars, too many strip joints, too many places to score a cheap drink or your drug of choice. Hell, you could even buy liquor in a plastic cup from bars right on the street and walk around with the booze in your fist.

With a saucy smile Gillian started up a conversation with the woozy duo. It didn't take long before she'd struck up a deal with one of them. As Alex watched in horror, she strolled out of the bar with the guy.

He cursed under his breath. He'd already taken one unauthorized break that evening. He should stay at his post until closing time. But he was damned if he was just going to stand here worrying about Gillian.

Daring Jack to stop him now, he walked to the back again, then hurried around to the street, thinking that he'd like to throttle Gillian Seymour.

Chapter Two

Outside, noise and heat and the smell of the nighttime crowd enveloped Gillian. But it wasn't the crowd that worried her. The look in Alexander McMullin's eye had curdled her stomach. And he wasn't her most pressing problem.

That would be the inebriate with his hand on her arm, a hand that was inching toward her breast.

"Come on, sweetheart, let's go back to my hotel room and have some fun." The invitation was issued in a drunken slur.

"I'm sorry I gave you the wrong impression," Gillian answered, politeness taking over from her former party-girl persona. "But I have to go home to my sick mother."

The man's hammy hand tightened on her arm and he leaned forward, his bourbon breath almost choking her. "You said you'd put out."

In her peripheral vision, she could see several spectators taking in the little drama. But nobody sprang to the aid of a working girl.

When the bad actor dug his fingers painfully into her flesh, she came down on the toe of his shoe with one of her stiletto high heels and he yelped, letting go of her arm.

"You whore! What the hell do you think you're doing? We had a deal."

"I'm an independent contractor and I can choose what jobs to accept. If you can't behave yourself on the street, what are you going to do in a hotel room?" she asked.

He blinked at her, apparently sobering up quickly. But before he could answer, she dashed away, hoping nobody in the crowd was planning to follow her.

Her first night as a prostitute, and she'd blown it. Well, not exactly, she corrected, cringing at her choice of words.

She sent an invisible dagger in the direction of Lieutenant LeBarron, who was probably home in bed at this very moment.

From the second she'd come under his command, he'd taken an interest in her career, which meant he'd urged her to grab this "choice" assignment.

It wasn't easy being a female cop in a big-city police department. The guys forced you to prove yourself—over and over. You had to shoot better than they did. Hold your own in hand-to-hand combat and stand up to their locker room comments. This assignment was a chance to show what she could do. And to shut off the supply of a dangerous new drug threatening the health and welfare of her city. Category Five was what they were calling the highly addictive drug that they suspected was being riddled by prostitutes to increase their business.

Truthfully, she'd been nervous about playing her assigned role, which was why she was out here tonight— practicing.

She'd known that a supersecret government agency called the New Orleans Confidential was teaming up with the N.O.P.D. for this operation. She hadn't known that Alexander McMullin was working for that agency. But there was no other explanation for his presence behind the bar in Bourbon Street Libations. She knew the man pretty well. He was a straight arrow and he certainly wasn't working as a bartender because he liked mixing drinks.

Once, when she'd been in a squishy, sentimental mood, she'd looked up his name in a baby book. Alexander meant "Great Protector." It fit. Except where she was concerned. He'd sworn to protect humanity. With a capital H. The big picture. He just wasn't too good when it came to relationships with women.

As she headed for the darkened side street where she'd parked her car, she found there was no way to avoid thinking about him.

"Damn you!" she muttered, then pressed her hand against her mouth. Mom hated cursing, and she rarely indulged in bad words, even mild ones.

But apparently Alexander McMullin brought out the worst in her.

As he'd stood with the solid barrier of the bar between them, she'd felt those blue eyes of his pierce all the way to her soul. And she hadn't liked the sensation. Because it made her feel as though she was back where she'd been two years ago.

For long stretches of time, she'd been able to forget about him. Then he'd come leaping back into her mind. Something as simple as a whiff of spaghetti sauce could do it. He hadn't been much of a cook, but that had been his specialty.

He'd said one of his stepmothers had taught him to make it. When she'd asked how he'd had more than one—he'd clammed up. Which wasn't unusual, because he never talked much about his family. Except another time when he'd said he'd arrested one of his half brothers. For carjacking. From what she gathered, he hadn't gotten his values from his parents or siblings. And, as far as she knew, he tended to avoid them. And long-term commitments, as well.

She grimaced. Two years ago he'd broken her heart. And she damn well should have known better.

They'd had a relationship that had been as fast and furious as it had been passionate. And then he'd told her it wasn't working for him.

Before they'd dated, she'd heard a lot about Alexander McMullin. He was tall of body, lean of hip, a real heartbreaker with wavy jet-black hair, a firm jaw and sensual lips. Other women she'd known had gone out with him. And the relationships had always ended the same way. If he was interested in you, he gave you the big rush.

Then he left you with your head spinning, wondering what went wrong.

She'd boldly told herself that she was the woman who was going to change things. For a while she'd dared to hope that she was the exception to the rule. She'd lasted longer than his average. Over four months. But in the hidden depths of her soul, she'd been waiting for the crash. Still, it had been a bitter shock when he'd told her it wasn't working for him anymore.

After Alexander McMullin she vowed to be a lot more careful about getting involved with anybody. Unfortunately, since Alex there hadn't been many guys who'd made the cut.

As she headed back to her apartment on one of the less gentle side streets off St. Charles, she couldn't hold back a bitter laugh. In the next few weeks she was going to meet a lot of guys, but she was pretty sure none of them were going to be suitable marriage material.

Lord, what if Mom and Dad found out about her undercover assignment? They'd been upset enough when she'd worked as a cocktail waitress to pay her college tuition.

"Quit that job and do something respectable," she'd heard almost every week. How were they going to like hearing she was playing prostitute?

Well, she'd just have to make sure they never found out.

ALEX WOKE FROM A BAD dream, where he was shouting, "Where the hell are you going?" as Gillian Seymour disappeared into the fog.

Sitting up in bed, he ran a hand through his dark hair, then turned off the alarm before it could ring. The automatic coffeepot filled the house with the aroma of French roast, so he got up and ambled toward the kitchen.

After grabbing himself a cup, he leaned against the counter and took a sip.

He'd bought his traditional courtyard house in a foreclosure sale almost two years ago, not long after breaking up with Gillian, and he'd poured a lot of energy into making the rundown place into an oasis where he could walk inside the garden gate and shut out the world. It was proof that he could create a life for himself that had nothing to do with his miserable past.

He'd installed a flat-screen TV and a king-size bed in the bedroom, then remodeled the bathroom to include a huge soaking tub. After that he'd outfitted the kitchen with new appliances and tile countertops. He'd stripped and stained all the woodwork. And he'd refinished the floors himself.

Mostly he was content here. But seeing Gillian again had brought back the loneliness that he could usually hold at bay.

So he dealt with his negative emotions the way he always did, with heavy labor. This morning he started adding a better mix of soil to the garden. After an hour's early morning work, he cleaned up and went online to do some research before heading for the New Orleans Confidential headquarters on Tchoupitoulas Street, down near the river, where the rent was cheap and the buildings were rundown.

The cover for the operation was a trucking company called Crescent City Transports, and the location requirements had been very specific. Conrad Burke had needed two back-to-back warehouses—one where the main trucking operation was located. There was a fleet of trucks in the cavernous garage, a nicely appointed executive office complex and a secret entrance to the other building through the common wall.

Although only in business for a few months, Crescent City already employed fifty drivers who carted everything from fresh produce to small appliances around the city. Backing them up was an office staff of six—including Burke.

The New Orleans Confidential's secret headquarters were in the other warehouse around back, which also housed part of the trucking operation. But it was kept separate from the regular delivery service. Although the trucks driven by the special agents looked the same on the outside as the ones assigned to the regular drivers, the undercover vehicles were jammed with state-of-the-art electronic surveillance equipment.

There were many similar warehouses in the industrial area, so the new company fit right in. But, like the special trucks, the exterior hid a boatload of surprises. The interior was soundproofed and bug-proofed and hooked up to a spy network that included satellite feeds, access to the CIA intelligent computer system, and secret transmitters. The walls also hid a weapons room, a science lab, a communications room and an electronics room.

When he'd first come to work here, Alex had been impressed. Today, seeing the buildings brought back his anger of the night before.

"Get a grip," he muttered as he resisted the urge to slam the car door.

From the collection of cars in the small lot, he could see that Rich, Mason, Philip Jones and Seth Lewis were already on site.

There was no way of knowing whether Conrad had arrived since the director parked in the front and entered the secret headquarters from a locked door to his office.

Alex raised his face and stared into the lens of the security camera mounted over the entrance. In addition to taking his picture, it scanned his retinas, making sure he was authorized to enter.

When the computer inside confirmed his identity, the door lock clicked open and he stepped quickly through the door.

He headed directly for the conference room, then stopped short when he heard somebody inside mention the name "McMullin."

The speaker was Mason Bartley. While Conrad had still been working as a U.S. Marshal, he'd caught the bastard red-handed in a liquor store robbery attempt. Mason had a rap sheet as long as Conrad's arm, but the new head of New Orleans Confidential had seen his potential and had him released into the agency's custody. In exchange for putting this case to bed, he'd walk away with his freedom. At the moment, it sounded like he was trying to win points by ratting on one of the other agents—namely Alexander McMullin.

Eyes narrowed, Alex listened to the jerk's version of the events of the night before. If he hadn't known better, he'd have assumed they were staking out two different bars.

"So, I think you should know that he left his post twice

last night. And he barged into a fight at the door. If he's not careful, he's going to get his ass fired. And why is he late now?'' Mason pushed.

''Business,'' Alex answered.

Keeping his expression neutral and his temper under control, he stepped into the room, taking in the men seated around the conference table at a glance.

Mason's blue eyes glinted with defiance. He and Alex had disliked each other from the first. Now Alex knew the guy had been looking for an excuse to stab him in the back. And the events of the previous evening provided what seemed like a great opportunity.

Everybody else, including Conrad Burke, who sat at the head of the table, looked slightly embarrassed. The short, curly haired Philip Jones slouched down in his seat, almost disappearing from view. Seth Lewis rolled his broad shoulders and stretched out his athletic legs under the table, but he kept his eyes fixed on a point somewhere near the floor.

Alex liked these guys. Each had his strengths and weaknesses, but they were all top-notch agents and he'd trust any of them to guard his back in a firefight. Any of them except Mason Bartley, of course.

Now he was sorry the conflict between him and Mason was making them uncomfortable, but he was glad he'd walked in when he had.

It was Rich who spoke up. ''Well, the way it looked to me, Alex was doing the bouncer's job—while the guy was taking a break.''

Mason didn't back down. Raising his head, he gave Alex a direct look. ''What about when you disappeared down the hall a little later? You were gone for ten minutes.''

Alex fought the urge to cross his arms defensively over his chest. ''We've been waiting to catch Jack Smith making another move. Last night I saw him slip some white powder into a customer's drink. One of the businessmen who came in after that fight. Like Longbottom, he left with a prostitute. Why didn't you follow them?''

Mason's complexion turned a dull shade of red. "I didn't see Jack do anything.''

"Well, I was closer to him," Alex said, giving the excon a way to save face, when what he wanted to do was ask Mason why he hadn't taken a seat nearer to the bar. "Since I knew what he'd done, I wanted to see where the couple was going.''

"And?'' Conrad asked.

"They went around the corner, then inside the Mc-Donough Club.''

"Which is?'' Mason asked.

Conrad answered. "For years it was a prestigious men's club in the city. Recently, I heard it changed hands.''

"Yeah," Alex agreed as he took one of the empty chairs around the large conference table. "I did some research on the place this morning. That's why I'm a little late." He paused for a beat to let the explanation sink in, then continued. "I checked out the ownership on the city tax records. The deed is in the name of a Cynthia Dupré." He took out a photograph he'd downloaded of a woman with a rounded face and dyed blond hair who appeared to be in her mid-fifties.

Phil studied it carefully. "She looks familiar, but the name sounds wrong." He tapped his finger against his lips, looking thoughtful, and Alex waited for some bit of buried information to come out. Phil gave the impression of being an easygoing, fun-loving guy with no other purpose in life other than being a party animal. But he was sharp, and he'd been working around New Orleans for years. One thing he brought to the Confidential network was a working knowledge of most of the lowlifes in the city.

"Unless I'm mixing her up with her twin sister—which I don't think she has—she was arrested for running a house of prostitution. I recollect that she paid some bribes and got off with probation," he said.

"Very interesting," Alex murmured. "I also checked out the liquor license for the establishment. It's supposed to be a private club, bar and dining facility—with a small hotel upstairs. I'm wondering if the rooms are rented by the night or by the hour."

Rich laughed. "Good going, Alex. It looks like we need to do some digging into that place."

"Bartley, you get a report on my desk by tomorrow morning," Conrad said, giving the sour-faced agent some extra work to do.

Mason answered with a tight nod.

"Did you already discuss the Latin types who came in later in the evening?" Alex asked.

Rich nodded. "I followed them after they left the bar."

"Where did they end up?"

"In a stretch limo that looked way out of their price range."

"Oh yeah?"

"I'm going to talk to the rental company."

They discussed more of the previous night's activities. Then Conrad asked, "Is that it?"

Alex took that opportunity to say, "Not quite. I'd like to ask some questions about the liaison with the police department."

Conrad nodded.

"Last night a rookie cop named Gillian Seymour came into Bourbon Street Libations dolled up as a prostitute. I assume she's part of the undercover sting set up by the N.O.P.D. to help crack the suspected prostitution ring and

finger the drug distributor. She left with one of the patrons.''

''And?''

''She just graduated from the academy a few months
ago. She's too green for the job.''

''The police commissioner approves department personnel,'' Conrad said.

Alex was aware that the rest of the men around the table
were listening to the exchange with interest.

''You mean, the redhead?'' Rich asked.

''Yeah.''

''She looked nervous,'' Rich observed.

''She should have,'' Alex rasped.

Mason jumped in. ''You know her?''

Alex swung his gaze toward the ex-con, knowing he'd
made a strategic mistake. He should have waited to bring
Gillian up when he and Conrad could speak in private.
''Yeah.''

''I don't envy her the job,'' Mason said. ''Getting pawed
by horny guys can't be fun.''

''If she can't handle them, perhaps we can ask for a
personnel change,'' Conrad offered.

Oh yeah, Alex thought, suddenly struck with the perfect
way to get her off the case.

Two DAYS LATER, just as Gillian had been about to leave
the station house to go over to her mom and dad's for
dinner, she got a message from the lieutenant's office. It
seemed she wasn't off duty, after all. A training meeting
for her undercover assignment was scheduled at an apartment off Esplanade Avenue, the dividing line between the
French Quarter and the city's downtown Creole neighborhood.

She changed out of her uniform and into a conservative beige pantsuit with a navy blouse—something that shouldn't call attention to her on the street. Then she made a quick call to her parents, apologizing for canceling the evening. Already late, she tried to get to the meeting on time. But she had to fight traffic all the way from the station house. By the time she arrived in the area, the only parking space she could find was a block away.

It was getting dark as she hurried down the cracked sidewalk, all her senses on alert. And she found herself thinking about when she'd been a little girl and Mom had told her never to walk home from school alone.

If she'd been given the choice, she would have picked a better location and a better time. But that was simply par for the course. It went along with the serious second thoughts she was having about the assignment.

If anybody asked why she'd taken the undercover assignment, she could come up with some kind of idealistic answer. And it would have been true, as far as it went. She certainly wanted to help get that Category Five off the streets. But now that she had a little taste of playing prostitute, she wasn't so sure she could handle the role. And what made it worse was the knowledge that Alexander McMullin would be sitting there watching her. She could deal with the remarks she was getting from the guys at the station house, but McMullin was another matter. With him it was personal, because he'd make it that way.

What if she asked to be reassigned? Would that be a black mark on her career? Something that would follow her through the department for years to come?

The tight feeling in her chest that she'd been fighting since she'd left the station house suddenly threatened to choke off her breath.

She'd been trying to keep her mind off the specifics of the assignment. She had to face some nasty questions. For instance, how was she going to work as a prostitute for a couple of weeks without having real sexual encounters with any of the johns?

A vivid picture of herself and a man like the one from last night alone in a bedroom came into her head, momentarily distracting her from her surroundings.

Bad mistake, because in the next second she had the feeling that someone was watching her.

She quickened her pace, scanning the immediate area, seeing nobody on the street and hearing no sound. But she felt a sudden malevolent stirring in the air—just as a hand closed around her arm. Before she could blink, a man with considerable strength pulled her into the nearby alley.

When she tried to use her police department martial arts training, the assailant was one step ahead of her, as though he knew what she was going to do before her body moved.

Another hand clamped over her mouth at the same time her body was pulled backward against a hard male form.

Desperate to escape, Gillian tried to bite the assailant. But he had anticipated that move, as well. The only thing she accomplished was to dig her front tooth into her own lip. When she winced, he pulled her deeper into the shadows.

They were several yards from the street now and she cursed herself for getting into this situation. She tried another tactic, going limp in the attacker's arms. He was ready for that maneuver, too. When she tried to wrench away from him, he pulled her into the shadows, even farther from help.

Chapter Three

Beyond the iron gate of a courtyard, Gillian could see potted plants and a small gurgling fountain. It looked quiet and peaceful in the courtyard, a strange place for violence.

"Open the lock," a man growled, his mouth close to her ear, the low, intimidating timbre of his voice grating at her nerve endings. She understood that he was trying to frighten her. And she strove to keep her cool. That was difficult when she couldn't even see him.

But she knew he was big and solid and dangerous. And she sensed a simmering anger or some other dark emotion coursing through him.

Unfortunately she was pretty sure that in the first few seconds of their encounter, he'd evaluated her strengths and weaknesses.

She didn't want to go into that enclosed space with him, but she could feel something hard pressing into her back and had to assume he was holding a gun—and that he was prepared to use it. He could already have taken her purse, if that's what he'd wanted. A sick feeling rose in her throat as she thought about what he probably had planned for her.

With unsteady fingers, she fumbled for the latch.

"Hurry up," he growled.

She gritted her teeth and did as he asked. He shoved her

through, kicking the barrier closed with a decisive clank behind him.

She tensed, prepared to make her move. But again he was ahead of her. In one smooth motion, he reversed her position, whirling her around to face him.

She was primed to fight for her life or to keep from being raped. But as she caught sight of the guy's face, she felt as though a large animal had kicked her in the pit of the stomach.

"Alex," Gillian gasped, taking in the reality of the man in a split second, starting with the wavy jet-black hair and the piercing blue eyes that had bored into her in the bar. She'd been thinking about him only minutes earlier. Maybe, deep down, she'd known he might try something she wasn't going to like.

A few nights ago she'd been thrown off balance by the hard stare he'd aimed at her. He was having the same effect on her now. Well, it wasn't just from the way he was looking at her. This afternoon, it seemed he'd deliberately set out to scare the spit out of her.

She knew her own eyes hardened as she said, "Alex, you…creep. What in the Sam Hill do you think you're doing lying in wait for me?"

"Is that any way to greet your savior?" he asked, his voice low and even, yet the anger she had sensed earlier was still simmering below the surface.

He was angry? Yeah right!

He was also excellent at pushing her buttons. She'd be smart not to let him get to her. Yet too much had happened in the past few minutes for her to keep her cool.

"Savior—my posterior," she snapped.

He laughed. It wasn't entirely a pleasant sound. "I'm saving you from a life of prostitution."

"Get real."

"Okay. If you want to put it another way, I'm giving you an illustration of the dangers you're going to be facing—if you let Lieutenant LeBarron talk you into this job."

Lieutenant LeBarron. So he'd been poking into her chain of command. Who did he think he was?

A few moments ago she'd been questioning her ability to deal with the undercover assignment. Now all her determination and righteous indignation came bubbling to the surface. "Oh yeah? Well, I'm a key player in this operation and I intend to complete the job."

"A key player! Is that what the lieu told you?"

She felt her chin jut upward. "Yes."

"Well, you're not going to be a key anything if you end up dead in an alley. Which you could have if somebody else besides a fellow law enforcement officer had grabbed you."

She folded her arms over her middle. "You took me by surprise. And you're not playing fair. You've had the same training that I have. And you used it against me."

He ignored the second part of her objection and focused on the first. "That's the way it happens in real life. You don't get to pick the place and time where the bad guy is waiting for you."

"I know that." She yanked her gaze away from him and made a show of looking at her watch. "You'll have to excuse me, but I'm late for a training session now."

When she tried to brush past him, he put a restraining hand on her shoulder. "Yeah. It's already started. Let's go on to the next phase."

Her head came up and she stared at him. "What do you mean?"

"In case you haven't gotten the message, I'm your trainer for the afternoon."

"No."

"I'm afraid you don't have much choice. Of course, if you want to confirm that assignment, you can give Lieutenant LeBarron a call."

She thought about doing just that, but she was pretty sure it wouldn't do her much good. "No," she said again through gritted teeth. "I'll take your word for it."

"Then you're with me for the next few hours."

She wedged her fists on her hips. "What strings did you pull to get me into this position?"

He had the grace to look uncomfortable, then recovered quickly. "As you might have figured out the other night, I'm an integral part of this operation," he said, paraphrasing her previous statement.

"Which means what?"

He glanced over his shoulder. "It's an undercover operation. I'd rather not talk about it out here."

"But if you're in on it, then we're supposed to be working together! Not playing games," she added in a gritty voice.

"I'm not playing anything," he snapped. "If you got exposed and interrogated, you can't blab what you don't know."

Interrogated! She tried not to think about the implications of that.

"We're going to be working together, so we might as well get comfortable with each other," he said in an easy voice. But she was sure his apparent conciliatory demeanor was just an act. Both of them knew there was no way for them to be comfortable with each other. Not with pictures flashing in her mind of the hot and steamy sex they'd enjoyed before he'd ended the relationship. Was he thinking about that, too?

He was walking in front of her now, so she couldn't see his face, and she didn't like the eager way he crossed the courtyard, his footsteps echoing on the paving stones. Just what did this training session involve?

She figured she'd find out soon enough as he pulled a key out of his pocket and unlocked a door on the far side. When she glanced at the number over the door, she noted that it was the address where she'd been told to report.

He paused and looked back over his shoulder. Managing a casual shrug, she followed him inside.

Alex led her into a dimly lit chamber. As soon as she'd cleared the door, he reached behind her and pushed it firmly shut. The sound of the lock turning was like a gunshot in the confined space. The drapes were drawn. Ignoring her, Alex moved several feet farther into the room and switched on a table lamp. In the warm glow from the light, she glanced nervously around the confined space and saw a chair, a chest, a night table. They were battered and old, like the furniture in her parents' house. But this room lacked any of the warmth her mom had given their home. And the piece of furniture that dominated the room was a double bed covered with a dingy chenille spread.

It registered then that she and Alex McMullin were alone in a very small bedroom.

"I thought we were going to go over self-defense strategies," she blurted, the words difficult to pronounce because her mouth was so dry. "This isn't supposed to be anything sexual."

He turned back to face her, looking her up and down, his gaze pausing at her breasts and then rising to her face again. "Well, there are two answers to that implied question," he said as though conducting a lecture at the police academy. "First, you are playing the part of a prostitute. So, by its very nature, your assignment has sexual implications. And second, as I said, the two of us have to be comfortable with each other. Depending on how things shake out, you and I could easily end up in bed together.''

The implications of point two had her reacting instantly. ''Now wait a minute!''

''I mean, we might have to act like we're on very friendly terms,'' he said smoothly.

As he spoke he took a step closer to her and she struggled not to back up. He was right, but she was pretty sure there was no way in hell she could act like she was pleased to be around him.

He stopped a few inches from her, well inside her comfort zone. Reaching out a hand, he stroked his finger lightly up her arm. Under any other circumstances, she would have turned him in for sexual harassment. But the assignment had given him the right to step over the line. Or had it? She wasn't thinking too clearly because her reaction was instantaneous. A shiver went through her body, quivering in all the sensitive places, and the only thing he'd done was touch her with one finger.

It took all her concentration to keep from looking down to see if her tightened nipples were poking out the front of her suit jacket. At the same time, she couldn't bring herself to meet his gaze. His hand dropped away from her and she saw him press his fingers against his thigh. She wanted to take that as evidence that the touch had affected him as startlingly as it had affected her. But she knew that her assumption would never stand up in court.

For several heartbeats, neither one of them moved.

Finally, Alex cleared his throat. ''So, you joined the N.O.P.D.''

''Yes.''

''Why?''

Keeping her features even, she scrambled for something that would sound like the truth. Certainly she didn't want to admit that it had made her feel closer to him. That would be much too revealing. And she didn't want to say that his idealism had rubbed off on her. She settled for, "It was a way to better myself."

He made a snorting sound.

She reacted with an angry question. "What's that supposed to mean?"

"Nothing."

"Wait a minute. You can't say that your reaction was nothing."

"You could have done better."

"How?"

He crossed his arms. "You got yourself a college degree. There are lots of jobs."

"What—were you checking up on me?"

He flushed, then recovered. "You don't get into the police academy without a degree."

She was still thinking about his response when she answered, "In case you haven't noticed, the job market sucks. There aren't a lot of terrific positions out there for college graduates who don't go further in school. I could have gone back to being a cocktail waitress. Or I could have accepted a red-hot offer to sell copy machines. Both of those were dead ends."

He slipped his hands into his pockets. "So you like playing prostitute?" he asked.

She knew he was baiting her, but she couldn't stop herself from trying to explain. "Of course I didn't join the police force to be a prostitute. But I can't say I'm ashamed to be involved in this task force. It's a good opportunity for me," she said, repeating what Lieutenant LeBarron had said to her.

"Have you told your parents about this assignment?"

"Now wait a minute! That's none of your business."

"You haven't."

"And don't you dare blab to them," she said, punching out the words. "Maybe I can't get you for sexual harassment. But if you mess with my family, I'll report you."

They glared at each other across several feet of charged space. Then his expression softened. "You always did protect them, didn't you? Like you never introduced me to them."

He made it sound as if she'd been ashamed of their relationship. That hadn't been it at all. If she'd taken him home, Dad would have seen that she'd been gaga over Detective McMullin. And she'd wanted to hide her feelings from them.

"Actually, I was protecting *your hide*. I didn't want Dad to go gunning for you after we broke up."

"Good point," he muttered.

To her relief, he stopped asking personal questions and made another quick change of subject. "Maybe you should get into uniform."

Turning away from her, he walked to the closet and opened the door. Inside were various garments draped over hangers. As far as she could see, none looked like police uniforms. The colors were flashy, the fabrics slinky. And her stomach clenched as she watched Alex slowly sort through the clothing, stopping to stroke his fingers over a skimpy knit top.

She wanted to protest when he pulled out a short shirt and transparent top, which he examined with interest. When he put them back, she breathed out a little sigh.

Her nerves jumped again as he fingered a lime-green dress—if that's what it could be called. The skirt was so short that it looked too skimpy for a skating outfit. And the low-cut bodice was adorned with large shiny buttons.

Alex held it toward her. "I'd like to see you in this."

"No."

He tipped his head to one side, regarding her with a deceptively bland expression. "What do you have against putting this on?"

"It's indecent."

"Yeah, that's right. But it's no more indecent than last night's fetching little outfit."

"Right, but I don't have to put it on in front of you now."

"I beg to differ. We're having a training session. Your life may depend on what you learn here today. Therefore, you'll comply with my orders."

"You're ordering me to put that on?"

"Yes."

She could have kept arguing. She *wanted* to keep arguing. She wanted to tell him that the charade was over. She had half a mind to call LeBarron to ask how Alexander McMullin had ended up being the boss of her. But if she didn't like the answer, she would be in a worse position than she was now. And she wasn't going to let Alex come out on top in this encounter. If he was determined to have her looking like a whore while they were alone in this room, then she was going to comply.

"I assume I don't have to change my clothes in front of you," she snarled.

"Of course not," he answered mildly.

"Good." Snatching up the outfit, she stomped past him and into the bathroom. She might have slammed the door, but she thought better of that act of defiance. She was going to keep this on a professional level if it killed her.

After closing the door quietly, she took off her jacket, then started to pull her knit top over her head. Instead she turned and glanced back toward the bedroom. Maybe getting undressed in here without turning the lock would be her first mistake.

Certainly it would make her vulnerable to the man waiting for her. Determined to show him that she was aware of safety precautions, she clicked the lock, pretty sure that Alex had been listening for that small sound. She clamped her teeth together, then deliberately unclenched her jaw. Closing her eyes, she tried to imagine what she would feel like if some other man were out there in the bedroom.

She'd be nervous and embarrassed. But not to the degree she was now. Alex was the reason she was reacting so strongly.

"Are you still alive in there?" a voice called through the door. His voice.

"It's not so easy to get into this outfit," she answered.

"Hmm. Maybe we should talk to the wardrobe department. Guys are going to be disappointed if it takes you forever to get naked," he answered.

She pulled off her blouse and slacks in record time. Just as quickly, she undid the gaudy buttons that secured the front of the slinky dress and pulled it over her head. The skirt was as short as she'd feared. When she looked over her shoulder, she could see her underpants in the mirror. Cursing under her breath, she tugged the skirt down, but that only made the vee at the front of the bodice worse. Working as quickly as she could, she struggled to do up the buttons. It was too tight across her breasts and too low to cover the tops. And the color made her look like a neon sign.

A pair of strappy high heels had been attached to the hanger. But there was no panty hose. Probably too inconvenient for quick sex. Since they were missing, she simply stepped into the shoes, then turned to face the mirror. A quick glance convinced her that she didn't want to take a closer look at herself.

Deliberately she made a mask of her features, then unlocked the door and stepped back into the bedroom. If she'd been planning to show how cool she was, Alex had completely foiled her effort. He was lying on the bed, his legs comfortably crossed at the ankles, his shoulders propped against the two pillows, looking relaxed and ready for whatever the evening would bring.

All that was bad enough. The fact that he'd removed his shirt and unbuckled his belt made the breath freeze in her lungs. She remembered lying in the circle of his large muscular arms. Remembered the tantalizing feel of the coarse dark hair on his chest against her breasts. "What are you doing?" she asked, hearing the breathy quality in her own voice.

"Getting comfortable."

"You're not supposed to be comfortable."

"I'm supposed to be pretending that you and I are in this room to have sexual intercourse. Or maybe I'm the kind of customer who's more interested in deep throat."

The way he said that made a shiver travel down her spine. That wasn't the only reason for the reaction. He was looking her up and down, taking in the green fabric stretched across her breasts and the way the short skirt brushed against her thighs. And from the look in his eyes, it was apparent that he liked the view.

"Come here," he said, his voice rough. That tantalizing grating sound gave her hope that he was as affected by this encounter as she was herself.

What if she played this sexy? What if she gave him a dose of his own medicine? As soon as the idea surfaced, she decided that it was much too dangerous. *He* was much too dangerous.

"Sit down," he said.

She might have defied him. Instead, to prove that she could handle a close encounter, she perched on the side of the bed. When he reached out and captured one of her wrists with his hand, she quivered.

"Jumpy?" he asked.

"No."

He laughed softly. "Sure."

"Why don't you get on with the training?" she demanded. "You don't have to show me how to have sex. So what's on the program?"

His hand tightened around her wrist. "You may be on this assignment for a few weeks. How do you plan to avoid doing the dirty with the guys who are paying for your services?"

Once again, her mouth was so dry that she could barely speak. When she licked her lips, she knew he was following the movement. "They told me there was something I'd be able to use. Some drug or something…" Her voice trailed off and she gave a small shrug. "But they haven't worked out the details yet."

He made a snorting sound. "An experimental drug. Oh great!"

"I have faith in the department."

"A long time ago, I did, too. And you probably heard what happened to me."

She knew he'd been burned out. She knew he'd quit. But she was just getting started and she wasn't going to let his cynical attitude poison her relationship with her bosses. "Don't try to undermine my resolve."

"Why not? Maybe you need a dose of reality."

"I need to keep my focus." She had been looking at his hand around her wrist. Now she raised her eyes to his and saw that he was watching her with burning intensity.

She almost lost her nerve, but she kept her voice even as she said, "Alex, I accepted this assignment, and I need to do well. For my own sake as much as for anything else."

His face turned hard. "Did some jerk give you a hard time?"

She wanted to tell him that the jerk had been him. He'd dealt a killer blow to her self-esteem when he'd walked away from her. But she wasn't going to let him know that.

Instead she shrugged. "I've had my share of bad times along the way. You know how the men treat female cops. I'm always being tested, so I appreciate the chance to show I can handle a difficult assignment—and put some prostitutes and drug dealers where they belong. Your role isn't so easy, either. You're working as a truck driver during the day and tending bar at night."

It was his turn to demand, "Have you been checking up on me?"

"No more than you've been checking up on me. Actually, after I saw you the other night, it wasn't difficult to find out what you're doing. There's a lot of interest in you around the department."

The moment she'd said the words, she wished she could call them back.

His expression had turned fierce. "Oh yeah?"

She imitated his shrug. "You can't walk out on the N.O.P.D. and not expect people to be curious whether or not you landed on your feet."

"More like, they want to hear I landed on my butt."

"No," she denied. But she knew that was partly true.

FOR A MOMENT Alex's mind drifted to the recent past. He'd made enemies when that murder case had gone sour, even though he'd done his job and never violated the chain of evidence. But somebody had screwed up. When he'd tried to find out who it had been, he'd hit a blank wall.

He pulled his attention back to the present, to the scantily clad woman sitting beside him.

He'd made an error in judgment inviting her onto this bed with him. And now he had to do something about that.

Focusing on her with laser intensity, he asked, "So what are you going to do if a john gets aggressive? What if he pulls a blade and gets ready to cut you up?"

She sucked in a sharp breath, he could see from her face that he'd hit a nerve. While he had her on the defensive, he reached under the pillow and pulled out the knife he'd hidden there when she was in the bathroom. It wasn't as sharp as it looked, but it could do damage, just the same.

In a quick motion, he brought it down toward her breast. To his vast relief, Gillian reacted instantly, chopping the side of her hand down on his wrist, making him wince as he dropped the weapon onto the spread beside them.

"Good going," he muttered.

"Did I hurt you?" she asked anxiously.

Machismo had him answering, "No." Although it was difficult to utter the syllable without wincing. Carefully he picked up the knife and slapped it onto the bedside table.

She was sounding a little cocky when she said, "What other nasty tricks do you have planned? By all means, bring them on."

He debated his options, thinking there were a couple of ways he could go. He was betting that if he wanted to, he could tie her up and do any damn thing he wanted. But he chose to give her a fighting chance. Or maybe he was the one who needed the chance.

"Okay. When a prostitute is with a john, he can request all kinds of sexual services. But the one thing he's not supposed to do is kiss her. What are you going to do if some bastard tries the forbidden?''

She opened her mouth to speak. But no sound came out. There was a charged moment when they stared into each other's eyes. He was thinking that he'd trapped himself. Then, without giving himself time to question his own sanity, he brushed his mouth against hers. It was only the barest contact, but it made him understand why kissing was forbidden commerce in the oldest profession.

His whole being absorbed the intimacy and the power of that simple act. He was instantly so hard that he was in pain.

He waited, his heart pounding, for her to give him a quick shove. That was what she *should* do, but she stayed where she was.

They'd come to this room as enemies, although neither of them had articulated that state of affairs.

Suddenly they were catapulted into another time and place as the well-remembered essence of this woman surged through him, overwhelmed him with the taste of warmth and honey and desire.

He was helpless to hold back the low sound of need that welled in his throat as he deepened the kiss. He had tried to forget the mind-blowing reality of kissing Gillian Seymour. But it had come flooding back before he could put up any defenses.

Slowly he experimented with remembered sensations, rubbing his mouth back and forth against hers, increasing the pressure, nibbling, taking her lip between his teeth, then plunging deeper into her mouth.

Somewhere in his brain he silently begged her to put a stop to what they were doing. But her arms only tightened around him.

The kiss went from heated to white-hot in the space of

heartbeats. Unable to stop himself, he angled his head, his mouth hungry and demanding, staking a new claim as his tongue slid against hers, tasting and stroking and stoking his arousal.

How could he have given this up? he wondered with the part of his mind that was still capable of putting one thought in front of another.

Perhaps it was the same for her. He hoped it was the same as he pressed her body to his, glorying in the twin pressures of her breasts against his chest.

He needed more. Yanking at one of the gaudy buttons on the front of her dress, he eased it open so that he could stroke the inner curve of her breast.

She made a small, gasping sound, fueling his need. He had told himself he could control his reactions, but suddenly it was impossible to deny himself the feel of her body against his aching erection.

Hastily he pushed the pillows out of the way, then wrapped his arms around Gillian and lay back, pulling her on top of him, sighing at the wonderful weight of her body pressing down on his.

Chapter Four

Alex had unzipped his fly before lying down. The move had been part of his intimidation tactic. Now it only provided a spur to his own out-of-control desires. It would be so easy to get out of his jeans, to get Gillian out of her panties. To plunge himself inside her. He knew exactly what that would feel like. Because vivid, erotic memories sang in his brain, making his whole body vibrate with the need to possess her again.

He was getting ready to roll her over and come down on top of her when he felt her body stiffen.

His eyes blinked open and he stared up at her, taking in the mixture of arousal and confusion on her face. That look undid him.

''Alex, don't. We can't.''

He wanted her with a passion that shocked him. And he was pretty sure that he could make her forget her objections by sealing his mouth to hers. Yet he knew in that instant he'd be making a serious mistake if he pushed her. Hell, he'd already taken a giant step down the wrong path.

He rolled to his side, easing her away from him. For just a moment he clasped his hand over her shoulder, then forced himself to break the contact.

Standing, he zipped his pants, fighting the erection that made it difficult to work the zipper.

"Sorry," he muttered as he shoved his arms into his shirtsleeves and started on his shirt buttons. "Things got a little out of hand."

She sat up, discovered that the top button of her dress was undone, and began to fumble with the closing. As soon as she was back together, her eyes shot to the door, and he knew she was wondering if she could get around him to make a quick escape. The panic on her face shook him to the core. He wanted to step aside, but she was hardly dressed for the street. Her skimpy outfit would only make her a target in this neighborhood.

"I'll clear out," he said in a rough voice. "Lock the door behind you."

Scooping up his shoes, he headed across the room.

Behind him, he heard her feet hit the floor. "Alex, we need to talk."

Not in this lifetime, he thought as he made a speedy exit from the training session that had gotten way out of hand.

He might have paused in the courtyard to put on his shoes, but instead crossed the paving stones in his stockinged feet. Ignoring the stares of several people on the street, he carried the shoes toward the delivery truck that he'd driven. How could he have left control like that? All he'd intended was to intimidate Gillian into dropping the task force, because it was simply too dangerous for someone he cared about.

The last part of that thought brought him up short. He didn't want to deal with it now. So he tried to focus his attention elsewhere. Gillian had stood up to everything he had thrown at her. But thinking about the two of them together inevitably dragged him back to personal matters.

Somewhere in the middle of the training session, he'd lost sight of his purpose. No, he'd lost his mind!

His foot came down on a piece of gravel and he snarled out a curse, knowing the pain in his foot was just an excuse to give vent to the chagrin and frustration he was feeling.

Once again, he went back to a mental exercise he'd invented: pulling up scenes from his past that made him a bad relationship risk—specifically for Gillian.

There were so many incidents to choose from. A good one that came to mind was the afternoon Barbara Wallings, his dad's third wife, had forgotten to pick him up after baseball practice. The coach had offered to give him a ride home. But he'd known that Barbara would be furious if she went to the trouble of showing up and he wasn't there. So he'd waited at the edge of the parking lot—in the rain. He'd stuck around for half an hour, then walked home, wet and bedraggled.

Barbara hadn't even apologized. In fact, she'd been angry that he'd gotten her kitchen floor dirty.

Or what about the time in middle school when the electricity had gone off? They'd sent all the kids home from school. He'd been the first one to walk into the house. When he'd heard moaning from the master bedroom, he'd found Cindy—his dad's fifth wife—in bed with another guy. Alex had backed out of the room before either one of them had noticed him.

He knew a kid with a whole drawerful of toxic memories wasn't going to make either a good husband or a good father. So he'd vowed he wasn't going to try at either.

With a feeling of resignation, he stopped to put his shoes on, silently wondering how he was going to face Gillian Seymour the next time they met.

"HEY, WHAT THE HELL do you think you're doing?" the guy packing up produce at the stall in the French Market shouted.

The girl with the long blond hair didn't answer. She simply closed her fist around the orange she'd picked up from the fruit bin and wove her way through the merchants closing up for the night.

"Voleur!"

He'd called her a thief. She knew that from French class.

The epithet rang out behind her, but she kept running into the side stands set up in the paved area beside the old market.

She rounded the corner of a booth bright with African print dresses, then slowed down, lest she call too much attention to herself. She could go back to the cheap motel where she was living. At least for one more day. She had enough money left for the night. Then she was on her own.

A spooky-looking man gave her the eye and she raised her chin and hurried on. She tried to look as though she were in control of her life. But she was seventeen and scared.

"Damn you, Daddy dearest," she muttered under her breath. "Why couldn't you just have been in town?"

She'd been counting on him to help her out when she'd arrived in New Orleans. But when had he ever come through for her?

She hadn't even seen him in a couple of years. He was always too busy. And she'd been okay with Mum, until last year, when she'd married again. Her husband, Marv, had turned out to have roving hands—and her home had turned into a nightmare.

She'd tried to tell Mum her new husband was a creep. But she hadn't listened. Or maybe she hadn't wanted to hear about it. Which meant that getting out of the house had been the only alternative.

So she'd raided the cash her mum kept hidden in one of her dresser drawers. It was a lot of money. Mum was stinking rich. And thank God she kept a bunch of American dollars around as well as British pounds. Enough to live for a couple of weeks in New Orleans, after she'd bought a one-way ticket from London.

She'd thought she could meet up with Dad here. But she'd found out soon enough that he wasn't home. And nobody could tell her when he was expected back.

Fighting the tight feeling in her chest, she decided she didn't want to be alone. So she headed back toward Jackson Square where the action was.

She'd made friends with some of the kids who hung around there. Most of them were living on the street. At first that had made her skin crawl. Now she'd decided that if they could do it, so could she. At least until Dad got back in town.

GILLIAN HAD WAITED with bated breath for Lieutenant LeBarron to ask about the training session. But he was busy with a spate of break-ins. So he didn't have time for her.

Still, she was on edge. She went out on routine patrols for the next few days. But the task force was always in the back of her mind. Especially after she'd gotten an official memo that she had been selected to work undercover in the bordello where the authorities suspected drugs were being distributed. Well, lucky her.

What did Alex think about that? Was he going to try to get her off the assignment again? His attitude was maddening. On the other hand, one thing she knew for sure now. He might have ended their relationship. But he still wanted her. Sexually. He'd proved that when the training session had gotten out of control.

She could make love with him again. That might feel

good—for a couple of minutes. But she knew it would leave her more humiliated than she'd been two years ago when he'd announced that they were through.

Finally, after letting her stew for days, LeBarron called her into his office. He was a blunt man with cropped hair, assessing gray eyes and a face that had once been lean. Now it was going jowly, to match the rounded paunch that had crept over the front of his belt.

"Sit down, Officer Seymour," he said, speaking formally. He was usually a bit distant in his verbal communications. But she had seen him eyeing her in a way that bespoke personal interest.

Conscious of his gaze on her, she sat in one of the wooden chairs across from his desk.

"We're getting ready to activate phase two of the task force," he told her. "Alexander McMullin has definitely identified the establishment where the prostitutes are taking their customers."

At the sound of Alex's name, Gillian unconsciously pressed against the chair back.

"When we first agreed to work with the Department of Public Safety, I wasn't so sure about McMullin. But he's provided some useful information.

"And Conrad Burke—who heads up New Orleans Confidential—is very pleased with his performance. He'll be briefing you on the parameters of the assignment. Also, their organization is handling security for you, so McMullin will cover that end as well."

She struggled to keep her expression neutral. "I thought he was working undercover tending bar at Bourbon Street Libations?"

"He's been reassigned."

You mean, he got himself reassigned, she silently corrected. For a split second she thought about saying she'd prefer to work with anyone else on the NOC team. But there was one thing she had learned quickly in the department: patrol officers didn't call the shots. They followed orders.

LeBarron gave her an assessing look. "If you're having second thoughts about going undercover as a prostitute, now is the time to say so."

She squared her shoulders. "I'm fine, sir."

"I know this will be a difficult assignment. But when I picked you, I thought you'd be up to the job."

"Thank you, sir. I am." She cleared her throat. "Can you give me any more details?"

The Lieu rocked back in his chair. "I'd rather let McMullin do that. You'll be meeting with him at 2100 hours this evening—at the surveillance van that will be monitoring you when you go into the bordello." He shuffled through the papers on his untidy desk, found the one he wanted and handed it to her. "Here are the particulars."

"Thank you, sir," she said again, rising, pretending that her stomach hadn't tied itself into knots. She resisted the impulse to clench her hand around the paper and crumple it into a ball as she turned and left the office.

Once in the hallway, she scanned the bold print. It noted the location where she was supposed to meet the van and stated that two officers would be assigned specifically to monitor her undercover activities. One of them was the man who had signed the letter. Alexander McMullin.

THE NIGHT had turned foggy, and as Gillian hurried down Chartres Street, she fantasized that the mist had swallowed up the van she was supposed to meet Alex in.

When she'd been a kid and Dad had driven her to school on foggy days, the landscape would be hidden by the white mist. Since she couldn't see the familiar stucco building, she'd always hoped that Warren G. Harding Elementary School had drifted into the twilight zone. But the two-story edifice invariably emerged from behind the obscuring curtain—just the way the white van materialized now on the next corner. There were no windows in the back and no side door. The entrance to the cargo area was at the rear.

The last thing she wanted to do was to climb into that van. But she didn't allow herself to slow her steps. Instead she walked up to the back door and knocked.

"Who is it?" a muffled voice called. The sound grated along her nerve endings. Muffled or not, there was no mistaking that it was Alexander McMullin.

"Officer Seymour," she answered.

"Just a minute."

She stood with her heart pounding, waiting for the door to open, wondering if he was postponing the moment when they had to face each other after he'd made a mess of that training session five days ago.

No, that wasn't fair, she told herself. It had been as much her fault as his. When he'd lowered his mouth to hers, she hadn't put up a fight. When he'd reached for her, she'd melted into his arms.

Her fists clenched and unclenched. She'd relived the heated encounter a thousand times. But she'd told herself she could keep the red-hot memory out of her mind when she met him again.

Now she knew she'd been lying to herself.

Finally the door opened and they stood regarding each other. There was a lot he could say now. So could she, but she kept her lips pressed together.

He cleared his throat and she waited for some kind of comment about the two of them. Instead he stepped aside and said, "Come in."

He was wearing jeans and a dark-colored pullover shirt, and unfortunately, he looked as good as she remembered.

Resolutely she reached for the edge of the door and pulled herself up. But nerves made her step unsteady, and she almost fell as her right foot came down on the rubbery surface of the van floor.

Alex's hand shot out and caught her upper arm, steadying her, sending a zing of awareness through her.

Quickly he pulled her into the van. Just as quickly, he took his hand away, so that she stood swaying slightly in the dimly lit interior, knowing that she hadn't been the only one to react.

She might have reached out to steady herself. But there didn't seem to be a suitable surface to use. Every inch of the interior of the truck was crammed with expensive-looking, hi-tech equipment that was covered with dials and switches that she was sure she shouldn't touch. She recognized several computers, television monitors, radios and other snooping devices—as well as stuff she couldn't identify.

"I thought there was supposed to be another guy working here with you."

"He's got the night off."

The statement hung in the confined space. Looking around, she asked quickly, "What is this, the Pentagon War Room?"

He laughed. "Close." His face immediately sobered. "This stuff might make a life-and-death difference for you."

She shoved her hands into the pockets of her jeans. "A nice way to put it," she muttered.

"I'm trying to get across the concept that we're not playing games here. Once you go into that bordello, this van will be your only means of calling for help."

"If I need it."

"Right. If you need it."

He gave her a tight nod, then walked to the front of the vehicle, sat down behind the wheel and started the engine.

"Where are we going?" she asked, sitting in the passenger seat.

"Not far."

She thought he might be heading for Bourbon Street Libations, but he stopped short of the bar and turned the corner, then gestured toward a large, stately-looking building.

"That's the McDonough Club, an established men's club for over a hundred years. Recently it was purchased by a woman named Cynthia Dupré. She runs the operation, but we know she must be fronting for someone else."

Gillian stared at the slivers of light at the edges of the window shades, wishing she could see inside. "*That's* the bordello?"

"Yeah."

"It looks elegant," she murmured.

"It is. Downstairs, businessmen and other upstanding types can relax and have a drink. If they want some intimate action with one of the hostesses, they have to rent a room in what's billed as a 'small hotel' upstairs."

Her mind conjured up vivid pictures of what went on in the upper reaches of the club. "How does Dupré get away with running a house of ill repute in the middle of the city?" she asked.

"Well, as you can see, the operation looks legitimate—if you don't poke into it too closely. And payoffs to the local cops don't hurt. When Chief Courville found out about it, he was mad as hell. But my boss persuaded him to go along with us and allow the bordello to operate until they can nail the drug dealers."

She nodded, taking it in.

Alex got up and walked to the back of the van, where he turned on several television monitors. "We had some guys from the power company down here to do 'routine maintenance work.' So we've already got cameras trained on the front door and the alley," he said, gesturing toward screens above the windshield.

She saw a view of the front door of the club.

"Nothing interesting right now. But we're hoping to get some pictures of city officials."

"Is that part of the mission?"

"Not originally. But it could be useful." He turned away from the screens. "Let's get back to you. Your first job will be to convince Madam Dupré to take you on," he said, keeping his voice businesslike.

"We've manufactured a background for you. I have the particulars, which you'll need to memorize before your first meeting with her. Basically, when she checks on you, she'll find that you've worked for the past several years as a very well-paid call girl. Your credentials are excellent. According to your résumé, you've serviced politicians, actors, lawyers."

"Do call girls have a résumé?" she asked in a steady voice, determined that he wasn't going to make her lose her cool.

"Not in so many words. But when Dupré checks some of your references, she'll find out that you're just great in the sack. A five-hundred-dollar-a-night pro." He held her gaze for several seconds, and she couldn't help thinking about the last man she'd been to bed with. In fact, it was Alexander McMullin. Lucky for her that her new employers didn't know how little experience she really had. And that wouldn't matter, anyway, she told herself. She wasn't going to do the deed with anyone—was she?

When she focused on Alex's voice again, he was saying,

"And the icing on the cake is a reference from a very high-priced escort service in town. The owner, Tammy Ray Kemp, owes the police a favor, so she'll say you worked for her. In fact, she's already put in a call to Madam Dupré, saying that you might be stopping by."

"Good," she answered automatically.

"I'm glad you approve, because once you get into that house you're going to be operating in an atmosphere of extreme danger," he said, enunciating each word carefully.

"Are you still trying to get me to back out?" she asked in an even voice.

"I'm just trying to make you aware of the reality of the situation. If anybody suspects you're in the McDonough Club as a spy, you will be eliminated. And I don't mean they'll toss you out on your ass. More like you'll end up at the bottom of the Mississippi River wearing cement boots."

Although her stomach clenched, she kept her gaze level. "I assume you're here because you have ways to protect me."

"Yeah, well, as you probably know, we'd prefer to have you wear a wire so we could monitor your whereabouts and contacts at all times. But due to the nature of your, um, *work,* it's too dangerous to attach a recording device on your body."

When his gaze focused on her breasts, she felt them tingle. Trying to ward off the sensation, she dug her fingernails into her palms. She didn't want to react to Alexander McMullin. But she didn't seem to have any choice.

He was speaking again, being deliberately raunchy.

"If some guy starts undressing you, it wouldn't be good if he found a wire attached to your boob. And hiding it in a body cavity isn't an option, either, for obvious reasons."

"I understand that," she snapped, thinking that there was

another important question she needed to ask. But they should finish with this topic first.

"The best we can do is bug your bedroom." He opened a drawer in one of the metal tables and brought out a small box, which he handed to her.

Determined to keep her hands from shaking, she removed the lid. Inside was what looked like an ordinary lipstick tube. And when she twisted the shaft, a bright red cosmetic stick emerged. It was short and stubby, as though it had been used for several months.

"The microphone is in the bottom," he said. "It's highly sensitive. It will pick up a conversation anywhere in the room, and I assume it will pass muster when your effects are checked. In an emergency you can turn it off by twisting the button."

"Okay. Good," she managed to say as she snapped the lipstick tube closed and put it back in the box.

He took the box from her and stowed it in the drawer, then turned to one of the consoles and began to explain how they planned to monitor the signal from her room. But his words were only a buzz in her head. She couldn't focus on radio signals when there was something that had been bothering her since she'd accepted the assignment.

"We need to talk about sex," she blurted.

"Aren't you interested in learning more about how the eavesdropping system works?" he asked, his back still to her.

"Yes. But the department said there was some drug I could use to avoid having sex with my…clients. Only nobody's told me how that's going to work."

She knew she'd revealed too much when he turned to face her.

"Again, it's not the perfect solution," he said.

"Just give me the details," she almost shouted, then made an effort to look more calm.

Crossing the small space, he opened a drawer and took out another box. This one was larger and contained two items. One looked like a jar of face cream. Along with it, was a bottle that read Multivitamins. "This is a two-part system," he said. "The cream is an amnesiac. Have you ever had an operation, and they put you to sleep? Then when you wake up, you don't remember anything past counting backward from one hundred to ninety-seven?"

"Yes. That happened when I dislocated my shoulder during a soccer game in high school."

"I didn't know girls played that rough."

"Mary Lou Winstead did. Anyway, whatever they gave me made me forget about the whole experience of getting the joint put back in the socket."

"Well, this stuff has a similar effect. And it has the added benefit of opening the person getting it to subliminal suggestions. The delivery system is ingenious. You scoop out about a half teaspoon of the stuff and rub it on the guy."

"Where?" she asked, then wished the question hadn't leaped into her mind. From the way Alex tipped his head to one side and stared at her, she was pretty sure they were both thinking about the same body part. But his answer was mercifully straightforward.

"It doesn't have to be an intimate place. It can be anywhere you want."

"You mean, like his neck? His arm?"

"Yeah, that will work. It will put him to sleep in about five minutes. Maybe you can tell him you're giving him a massage to relax him. When he starts waking up a half hour later, you whisper in his ear that his performance in bed was fantastic. And he'll believe you."

"And how do I stay awake while the guy is nodding off, if I've got the same stuff on my hands?"

"An excellent question. You take your vitamins. They've got an ingredient that will block the anesthetic. But you've got to take the antidote at least fifteen minutes before you use the cream—to be sure you don't put yourself to sleep."

Relieved to finally have the details, she asked, "How long does the counteragent last?"

"Eight hours. That should get you through the evening. Or you might have to take another dose."

"Okay, good." She took a step back and waved her arm, trying to ease some of the tension coursing through her. Unfortunately her hand hit a folder on the narrow desk bolted to the wall and papers cascaded to the floor.

"Sorry." Quickly she bent to pick them up. Since Alex had first helped her into the van, he had avoided touching her. But when his hand brushed hers, she felt another shiver of reaction go through her.

Casting her eyes down, she focused on the papers, shuffling them together. Mostly she saw closely spaced text. But one sheet caught her attention. On it was a picture of a scorpion.

"What's this?" she asked.

Alex's jaw tightened. "The mark of the devil."

"I beg your pardon?"

"Have you heard of a South American country called Nilia?"

"Yes. Aren't they having trouble with a rebel leader named…Gonzalez?"

"That's right. How do you know?"

"I read the news magazines. There was a story about him a few months ago."

"Well, Ricardo Gonzalez is also known as Black Death.

He's after the oil resources of his country. And he's willing to do almost anything to get them—like killing anyone in his way, women and children included.''

"What does that have to do with this operation?''

"Gonzalez is the reason the Department of Public Safety opened a confidential agency branch in New Orleans. He's sent rebels here for reasons unknown, but we suspect they're here to raise money to finance his operation. It's our job to track their movements to find out what they're up to. All the guys who work for him wear this scorpion tattoo.''

She made a sound of disbelief. "Isn't that pretty stupid of them? I mean, that tattoo makes them instantly identifiable. If they get caught doing anything illegal, they can't claim they were innocent bystanders.''

"Yeah, that's right. It also makes them absolutely ruthless. They'll do anything to keep from falling into the clutches of the law because they don't have an escape hatch. And if they lose their nerve and want to quit the Gonzalez organization, they're stuck. Their only option is to stand and fight.''

She thought about the implications. He was right. Those guys would be formidable opponents.

"That's what we're up against,'' Alex growled. "Guys who have no choice but to be absolutely loyal to a tyrannical boss.''

"I'll keep that in mind,'' she said tightly.

He gave her a direct look. "You sound pretty calm. What—do you have a death wish?''

"I can take care of myself.''

"Like when I came up behind you the other day?''

"You weren't exactly playing fair.''

She didn't know how the argument would have ended, but a flicker of movement on one of the television screens caught her attention. It was from the camera that was trained on the back door of the club.

A woman had come out of the building and was standing in the alley. She was turned toward the camera, and Gillian got a good look at her. She seemed to be in her fifties, with wavy hair dyed a soft blond, a full figure encased in a draped satin dress, and a rounded face that went from calm to fierce as she stared down the alley.

"That's your new boss," Alex said, his tone sharp.

"Madam Dupré?"

"Yeah."

Gillian watched her, thinking that she looked pretty hard and ruthless.

"You're late," the madam said, and Gillian realized there was also sound with the picture.

A man walked into the scene. She heard Alex suck in his breath. "Well, well. Jack Smith," he muttered.

"Who?"

"Don't you recognize him?"

Gillian studied the man. "The bartender from the other night?"

"Yeah."

Jack looked up and down the alley to make sure that he and Dupré were alone.

"You have some stuff for me?" he asked.

"If you have some money for me," she answered, her voice sharp.

He pulled several bills out of his pocket. She riffled through them, then opened her black leather purse and took out a plastic bag. Jack stuffed it into his pocket. The whole transaction was over in moments and the bartender disappeared into the shadows.

"Those are the kinds of people you want to live with for the next few weeks?" Alex asked.

"Of course not. Who would? But you aren't going to get me to back out," she said, her voice rising in the confines of the van.

Chapter Five

Just after Alex turned onto Tchoupitoulas, heading toward the Crescent City Transports buildings, a tractor trailer came around a curve too fast, forcing him to brake and narrowly avoid a collision. He hurled a string of curses at the driver, when what he really wanted to do was to take out his foul mood on Gillian Seymour.

She was the reason for his sleepless night. After his session in the van with her, he'd lain awake, his stomach churning. A double dose of the antacids he kept in the medicine cabinet hadn't helped.

He'd wanted to reach out and shake some sense into Little Miss Rookie Undercover Agent. She'd been trying to act so cool. But he knew she was scared. Any woman in her right mind would be. But he hadn't gotten her to admit it, even when she'd seen that scorpion picture.

He fought to repress a shudder. He was hoping she'd never encounter the thing in real life. That is, on the body of one of the very dangerous creeps who worked for Gonzalez. Like the Latin men who had made themselves at home in Bourbon Street Libations the week before.

Well, they didn't seem the type to frequent the upscale McDonough Club. But then, they hadn't seemed like the type to climb into a limo, either.

As he came around another curve, he slowed. He'd driven this particular stretch of Tchoupitoulas for weeks now and was aware of every pothole in the road and every feature in the warehouses and vacant lots that lined the stretch of roadway.

He passed the old washtub that had been sitting on the curb since Moses had come down from the mountain and headed for the weed-choked field enclosed by the crumbling brick walls of a partially demolished warehouse.

An abandoned car had been parked in the weeds about as long as the washtub. It was a rusted-out junker with the tags removed so nobody would know who'd dumped it. Today it had a friend, a late-model Toyota that looked like it might have been recently stolen.

From the road, the newer vehicle didn't appear to have been stripped. Maybe some kids had taken it for a joy ride and left it sitting in the weeds. But this was a pretty out-of-the-way location. How had they gotten back to civilization? And why had the latch on the trunk been popped?

Alex might have driven on by. An abandoned car wasn't really his business. But his cop's training wouldn't allow him to just let the mystery go.

Easing up on the gas pedal, he slowed, then turned into what had once been a driveway leading to a warehouse. Much of the structure had been demolished, leaving piles of old bricks and a roofless courtyard where the two cars rested, the newcomer's front end at an angle facing the wreck.

He pulled to a stop about eight feet behind the new car and sat for a moment, surveying the scene. Then he climbed out into the sunlight. The whole site seemed to be abandoned, but he supposed that somebody could always pop out from behind one of the still-standing brick walls.

His attention was focused on the cars in front of him.

He'd taken a couple of steps forward when the sound of tires crunching over rubble alerted him to the fact that he was no longer alone. Cursing his own stupidity, he whirled around to see that another car had pulled in behind his, effectively blocking his exit from the area.

He would have reached for his Glock, but he wasn't wearing it. Protocol for his undercover assignment dictated going without a weapon.

So he stood with his muscles tensed as he waited to find out who had blocked him in.

The man who climbed out of the car was solidly built and over six feet tall with silver-gray eyes and thick chestnut hair.

Tanner Harrison's voice was conversational as he asked, ''Need some help?''

''What are you trying to do—give me a heart attack?'' Alex countered. He'd been so focused on the truck and then the newly abandoned car that he hadn't even known the other confidential agent was behind him.

''Nah. Just testing your reflexes. I timed your turn at under a tenth of a second.''

Alex laughed. ''Yeah. I thought you were out of town.''

''Just got back. But there's some repair work being done on my house, so I'm over at the Sheraton on Canal Street. What have we got here?'' Tanner asked.

''A vehicle that wasn't here yesterday afternoon.''

''Mmm, hmm.''

They both approached the car. Alex reached for the trunk, then stayed his hand. The buzzing of flies and the smell coming from the crack between the lid and the car body suggested that he wasn't going to find a couple of cases of beer inside.

Tanner was getting the same signals. Backing away, he

searched the ground, picked up a stick and used it to raise the lid.

Alex was pretty sure what he was going to see. His first dispassionate observation was that the sun beating down on the metal of the car hadn't done the body sprawled inside any good. But then neither had the slash marks crisscrossing his naked chest. Somebody had taken a lot of pleasure and pride in carving him up. And Alex could make a pretty educated guess about who the butcher was.

"It appears he pissed somebody off pretty good," Tanner muttered.

"The Cajun mob," Alex answered. "The knifework looks like it was done by Tony Arsenault—aka Tony the Knife."

"You've run into him?"

"Not face-to-face. But I know he's an enforcer for them. Well, I can't prove it. He's a careful bastard, and nobody's been able to pin a murder on him yet. But the P.D. is working on it."

They both stared at the body. The guy had dark hair and a tough-looking face. Below his naked torso, he was wearing casual slacks. One of his large hands was turned up and Alex leaned closer, then cursed.

"What?"

He pointed at the fingertips. "Somebody gave him an acid manicure. I guess they don't want any fingerprints."

Tanner studied the hands. "Yeah. A nice touch. It's gonna be tough to figure out who he is."

"Unless maybe he's got a scorpion tattooed on his back."

Tanner's head whipped toward him. "You think?"

"No, I just had those guys on the brain when I pulled in here."

Stepping back, Harrison pulled out his cell phone and

called the cops. When he finished, he looked at Alex. "They're sending a couple of dicks. They want us to wait."

"That's going to play hell with your delivery schedule."

"You're not on truck driver duty today?" Harrison asked.

"Not for a while. I'm going in to pick up my surveillance van. The P.D. recruit is having her job interview with the madam this afternoon." Alex kept his voice neutral, hoping Tanner didn't pick up on his tension.

Switching the subject abruptly, the other man asked, "So what do you think? I mean, why is this body down here?"

"You mean, did somebody leave it where a Confidential agent driving to work would find it? As a warning, maybe," Alex replied.

"Yeah."

"That's a possibility. Or this is just a convenient dumping ground. And they're gonna wish they picked a different spot."

The conversation was interrupted by the sound of a siren. Both Alex and Harrison pulled their vehicles to the side to give the team from the P.D. access.

THERE WAS ONE THING to be thankful for, Gillian decided as she reached for the jacket of her expensive, formfitting silk suit.

At least Alex hadn't made some grandstand play to prevent her from showing up at the McDonough Club.

Adjusting the jacket, she inspected her image in the mirror. She looked demure on the outside, but underneath was a different story. This woman was nothing like the tarted-up working girl who had come marching into Bourbon Street Libations the week before. No, this woman was sleek and sophisticated on the outside. Which made her role that much harder to play because her early life sure hadn't prepared her for sleek and sophisticated.

Forty minutes later she got out of a cab in front of the McDonough Club and paid the driver.

She squelched the impulse to wipe her sweaty palm on her slender skirt, then started up the steps of the large, well-kept building. Apparently it was like her suit, deceptive on the outside. From the sidewalk, it looked like a bastion of the old-money establishment in the city. But inside was a whole different story.

Although she was facing the wide double doors, she could see a delivery van around the corner. Probably the same van where she and Alex had met a couple of nights ago. So was he in here, already watching out for her? She hated to admit that she took some comfort in knowing he was here. Alex would come rushing in if he thought she was in trouble. She had the lipstick microphone in her purse. He'd be able to listen in on her conversation with the madam—and anything else that happened while she was near the hidden microphone. She would have liked some privacy for this interview, because she didn't love the idea of his critiquing her performance. But that was preferable to her going in here and never coming out again—with nobody knowing why.

That wasn't going to happen, she told herself firmly. Still, she had to repress a shudder as she raised her hand and clunked the ornate brass knocker shaped like an alligator head. A nice touch, she thought. Had it come with the property or was it new?

Gillian had picked her time carefully. She hadn't wanted to arrive too early because she expected that most of the women who lived here—Madam Dupré included—slept late. But she hadn't wanted to interfere with the evening's activities, either.

So it was just two in the afternoon. Still, the fit-looking man who answered the door was wearing a tuxedo, which failed to conceal the bulging muscles under his jacket.

"May I help you?" he asked. The question was polite enough, but she knew he was looking her over carefully, evaluating her purpose in coming.

"I'm Gillian Stanwick," she answered. "I believe Mrs. Dupré is expecting me."

He ushered her into a wide front hall where what looked like an antique sideboard competed for attention with a gorgeous Oriental rug and a man's marble bust sitting on a waist-high pedestal. Probably the founder of the club, she judged, remembering the photographs she'd seen of McDonough.

"Please wait here," he said, indicating a small room to the side of the entrance. Again, the furnishings were lavish. And the raised ceiling panels were painted gold. Like something out of an old plantation, she thought, remembering some of the field trips she'd taken as a kid.

She'd come from a working-class neighborhood, but the teachers had wanted the students to know about the former glories of their home city.

Instead of sitting, she inspected the titles of the volumes in the floor-to-ceiling shelves along one wall. Some of them looked like classical literature, but she was startled to see naughty-looking titles among the more staid offerings. You could read anything from the complete works of Charles Dickens to *The Tale of a Fallen Woman* or the *Bitches of Westwick*.

The sound of footsteps in the doorway made her turn quickly. The strong-armed but very polite butler—or whatever he was—had come back.

"This way," he said, ushering her down the hall toward the back of the establishment.

She concentrated on keeping her face serene as she followed him around a corner.

A young blond woman wearing a flowered dressing gown and carrying a mug of tea or coffee was coming down one of the side halls. She stopped short and gave Gillian an appraising look but said nothing.

Gillian replied with a small nod, then almost bumped into the butler's back as he stopped in front of a wide door.

"Come in," a woman's voice called in answer to his discreet knock.

"Miss Gillian Stanwick to see you," he said as though he were ushering her into the presence of British nobility.

He stepped aside and Gillian walked into the room, ordering herself not to flinch when the door closed tightly behind her.

The woman was seated at an old-fashioned desk, the surface of which was as neat as a prop in a furniture showroom.

She was the same woman in her fifties with dyed blond hair they had seen on camera the night before. Then she'd looked impatient and angry. Now she was obviously making an effort to school her plump features into pleasant lines.

"What can I do for you?" she asked, looking Gillian up and down as though she were in the grocery store evaluating a prime steak. Since she didn't offer her guest a seat, Gillian stood with her hands at her sides, hoping she didn't look like a marionette waiting for the puppeteer to jerk her strings.

In the van, after they'd observed the meeting with Dupré and Smith, Alex had given her more equipment and more information. He'd told her what to expect in this interview, and now she couldn't help picturing him sitting at his console critiquing every word she said and every move she made.

"I believe Tammy Ray Kemp told you I would be stopping by."

"Tammy Ray. A lovely girl. She used to work for me before she went into business for herself."

"Yes."

Madam Dupré continued to study Gillian. "I'm sure she wouldn't have sent you to me if she didn't think you'd qualify. But there's no point in interviewing you if you don't meet the physical specifications. We are very select here in our choice of girls."

"Of course."

"Please take off your jacket. And your skirt, so I can get a look at you."

IN THE VAN, Alex sat with his eyes glued to one of the television monitors. It was trained on the front door of the McDonough Club. And the picture hadn't changed in the past fifteen minutes. Not since Gillian had gone inside and the big guy in the monkey suit had closed the door, shutting her away from the world.

But he knew Rich Stewart was watching him and listening to the conversation inside through another set of earphones, and Alex didn't want to give away the fact that his stomach was so tied in knots that he might never eat again.

So he sat trying to act as though this was just a routine stakeout when the words he was hearing made him want to jump out of his chair, charge across the street and pull Gillian out of that place.

The madam had just asked her to strip to her underwear—right there in the office. He'd been waiting for that order. Probably, Gillian had, too. He was rooting for her to refuse. Then this whole charade would be over. Instead he heard her say, "Certainly." Her voice sounded detached, as though she were getting ready to execute a school assignment.

"I'm glad I'm not in her shoes," Rich murmured.

"Yeah," Alex managed to say through parched lips. He'd made the mistake of bringing up Gillian's name in the meeting last week. Now he knew that, like everyone else, Rich was curious about their relationship. But he wasn't going to enlighten him. He was going to keep his cool as he imagined Gillian taking off her clothing in front of that malevolent toad of a woman.

Rich cleared his throat. "We've got an excellent sound level from that mike."

Alex could only manage a grunt.

COOLLY, GILLIAN SET HER purse on the needlepoint cushion of a nearby chair. Then, pretending her fingers didn't feel numb, she slipped open the buttons of the jacket and took it off, laying it beside the purse. She'd dressed carefully for the occasion. Underneath she was wearing a sheer camisole and nothing else. Next she unzipped her skirt, revealing lace bikini panties, a white garter belt and flesh-colored stockings. Very aware that her body was on display through the almost-translucent underwear, she stood with her arms at her sides, facing the madam. When Dupré twirled her hand, Gillian turned slowly around, then came back to the starting position.

"Very nice," the older woman said. "Now just lift those nice breasts in your palms for me and stroke your fingers over the tips."

Gillian wanted to focus her gaze on the wall in back of the woman. Instead she deliberately made eye contact as she complied with the request. She managed to hold the woman's gaze, but her mind conjured up another scene.

Inside her head, she was pretending that it was Alex who was touching her as she felt her nipples harden.

Gillian forced herself to keep breathing evenly—in and out, in and out. And forced herself not to ask if she'd passed the test.

"Very nice," the madam said again. "Your figure is good. And you seem comfortable with displaying your body. You can put your jacket and skirt back on. Sit down and we'll talk."

Gillian reached for the skirt, gracefully stepping back into it and pulling up the zipper.

"How long have you been working as a prostitute?" the madam inquired as the would-be new hire buttoned her jacket.

Using the scenario she'd been given, Gillian was ready with an answer. "Two years."

"Why?"

She delicately lifted one shoulder. "The pay is good. The work is easy. I'm not going to be doing this for the rest of my life. I'm saving up to buy my own business."

"What kind of business?"

"A dress shop, catering to rich women who will never suspect that I bought my way into respectability by screwing men like their husbands."

The madam laughed, the sound like breaking glass. "A very elegant plan. But why do you want to work for me? You won't be making as much as if you were out on your own."

"That's true. But I had a little trouble with the cops. I've researched your house, and I understand you can offer me a pleasant and secure environment."

"And I'll take thirty percent of what you make with each john."

Gillian pretended surprise. "That's a little high."

"As you say, I can offer you a secure and pleasant working environment."

Gillian looked down at her polished nails while she thought over the terms. "I can live with that," she finally said.

"If a patron wants to enjoy the favors of two females, how do you feel about working with another girl?"

The question was the first one that had really thrown her off stride. "I prefer entertaining my customers alone," she said.

"And if I insist you do an occasional threesome?"

"I guess I made a mistake in coming here," she said in a quiet but firm voice, then held her breath, wondering if she'd just blown the job interview. But teaming up with another woman would put her in a position she couldn't accept, not if she was going to avoid doing her job.

"I can work around that," the madam said. "There are other girls in the house who will be glad to take the assignment."

"Thank you," Gillian said, hoping that relief didn't flood her voice.

"But you'd better be good enough to bring in the big bucks on your own. What acts are you willing to perform?"

As Gillian coolly listed the usual sexual repertory, she couldn't help flashing on Alex again, picturing him glued to the conversation. Determinedly she forced him out of her mind.

"What if a client wants to be disciplined?"

"Whipped?"

"Yes."

"I can handle that. But I don't want to go the other way. I don't want to accept physical abuse."

"Again, we have other girls who enjoy it, so that won't be a problem."

Unfortunately that was probably true, Gillian thought. Then she brought her attention firmly back to the interview as the madam asked a question about her early life. Keeping her mind off her own warm and loving family, she mentally flipped through the pages she'd memorized and answered smoothly.

When they finished, Madam Dupré leaned back in her chair. "You sound like you'd work out very well here. But you understand that there will be a probation period."

"Of course."

"Do you have any questions?"

"Yes. How are payments from customers handled?"

"Discreetly. We take care of that for you. And a record is kept of your earnings. The money can be transferred to your account monthly."

Gillian nodded.

They went on to discuss some of the house rules. Gillian must be available for work every evening from seven on. She would have one day off each week, but in the beginning she would be expected to work the weekends.

"And finally, you will not be allowed to leave the house without asking my explicit permission. Frank, the man who showed you in here, will strictly enforce that rule. He has orders to be quite rigorous."

"Yes. I understand," she answered, glad the sleeves of her jacket hid the goose bumps that had suddenly risen on her arms. She'd expected that she wouldn't simply be allowed to waltz in and out of the place. But she couldn't help feeling the walls of the little room closing in around her.

The madam tipped her head to the side. "How soon can you start?" she asked.

"I was prepared to come to work this evening, if you

needed me that soon. But I do want to go home and get a few things. My makeup. Some working clothes."

"I have everything you need right here," Madam Dupré said. "You could just go in the back and meet some of the other girls. Then you could make yourself comfortable until customers start arriving."

Gillian fought to keep her face neutral. She hadn't brought her makeup kit along, and she needed it. Without the special contents, there was no way to keep from having sex with the men who came here. "I'll be more comfortable with my own things," she said, then waited with bated breath for the madam to seal her fate.

Chapter Six

"You can go home and pack," Madam Dupré said.

"Thank you."

"I want you back here within the next two hours," the woman added, her voice brisk now that she and Gillian had struck a deal. "And don't come in the front door again. There's an employee's entrance in the alley in back."

"Yes."

"Go down the hall and turn right."

Feeling as if she'd won a victory and at the same time sold her immortal soul to the devil, Gillian escaped from the little office. In the hallway, she let out a small sigh. She was waiting for the man called Frank to put a hand on her shoulder and ask her where she thought she was going. But she didn't see him around.

As she headed toward the right, she saw him at the end of the hall. He was talking to two women. Girls, actually. They appeared to be very young—and not happy to be in the house. One tried to brush past him, but he grabbed her by the arm and firmly turned her in the other direction. It looked like he was hurting her, or at least intimidating her. Was she here against her will? Had she changed her mind about working for Madam Dupré? Was she of legal age? All Gillian's training and instincts made her want to go to the kid's rescue. But she knew that her assignment came first. She'd just won herself a job here, and she had to keep it. So she headed for the back door and stepped out into the shadows of the alley, then circled the building and came out on the sidewalk.

When she emerged into the sunshine, she automatically looked down the block. Not seeing the white van brought a sudden pang. Had Alex abandoned her, after all?

Then the vehicle came around a corner and she sighed a breath of relief she hadn't realized she'd been holding. Of course, he couldn't stay in the same position for hours.

She could have gone in the other direction. Instead she walked toward the vehicle at a steady pace because she wanted Alex to know for sure that she was okay.

She didn't expect to actually see him. But when she was five feet from the van, the door opened and he stepped out. He was dressed in a brown uniform and was carrying a large box, as though he was getting ready to make a delivery. Their gazes locked and she felt as though they were silently exchanging a wealth of information. He looked relieved to see her. She probably looked relieved, too. And glad that he was there, although the embarrassment factor was stronger than she would have liked. She'd had a pretty intense sexual conversation with Madam Dupré, and Alex had been listening to all of it. And the madam had asked her to touch herself. What had he thought about that?

Well, it wasn't just Alex who had been listening in. Behind him, she could see another man standing in the doorway of the van, looking at her. She guessed he'd heard the whole thing, too.

She raised her chin just a bit, but she didn't stay to hear them critique her performance because she knew that somebody from the McDonough Club could be watching her. Or even getting ready to follow her. So she paused for only a moment before moving on down the block in the direction of the apartment that was supposed to be her home. It wasn't, of course. It was just a location the madam could check out if she was doing a background investigation of her new recruit. And when she did, she'd find that Gillian Stanwick had been renting the apartment for the past eighteen months. But she'd gotten behind in her rent and the landlord had asked her to leave.

GILLIAN WAS BACK at the McDonough Club in less than two hours, wheeling two large suitcases. Following directions, she pulled her luggage into the alley, then shifted her makeup case under her arm and knocked at the back door. This time a woman in a maid's uniform answered.

"My name is Wilma," the woman said. "The madam asked me to wait for the new girl."

"I'm Gillian Stanwick."

"That's a fancy name."

Gillian gave her a conspiratorial smile. "Yes. It's like a stage name, you know. I wanted something that sounded ritzy."

"Well, it does. I hope you think your room lives up to the name. I've gotten it all ready for you."

"Yes, thanks."

Wilma took one of the suitcases. Gillian took the other up a back staircase to another wide hallway that was papered in blue and cream with oil paintings in gilt frames on the walls, depicting old-time New Orleans and Louisiana scenes. Probably they'd been here when the building had really been a club. Gillian's room was number eight, halfway down the passage. The door was unlocked, and Wilma ushered her inside, standing back for her to get a good look.

It was pretty impressive, even by hotel standards. The space was large. And the furniture looked like real Victorian antiques, with a carved four-poster bed, a desk, a dresser, an armoire and two easy chairs in the bay window. The floorboards were wide and polished and partially covered by an Oriental carpet in tasteful blue and peach to match the spread and draperies.

Gillian set her makeup case on the dresser, then proceeded to the bathroom where she found a huge soaking tub, a separate shower and a marble sink counter.

"This is beautiful," she said to Wilma.

"Thank you," the maid answered as though she'd personally arranged the setting. Crossing to one of the bedside tables, she opened the top drawer. "There's a loose-leaf notebook in here that you'll want to read. It tells about the rules and services of the house. In case you don't get a chance to study it right away, you're supposed to be downstairs in the lounge by seven. Madam Dupré can get a little bent out of shape if you're late.

"And one more thing you'd better know. Your room must be neat and ready to receive company at all times. And if you want to have a bite to eat before you start work, you can come down to the kitchen. There is no eating in your room, unless a guest requests a private supper with you."

"Thanks for the information," she said, truly grateful for the quick summary. "What should I wear for the evening?"

"Something elegant and comfortable. But not too revealing. We have visitors in the bar area who are just using the facilities downstairs. If you don't have something suitable, there are outfits in the armoire."

Unlike Frank or the madam, the maid sounded friendly, but Gillian knew she had to be cautious with her—just like with everyone else here. So she offered the woman a ten-dollar tip, along with her thanks.

As soon as the door closed behind her, Gillian took off her jacket and started to drape it over the dressing table chair. Then she remembered the edict about keeping the room neat and went to the closet to hang it up. She removed her skirt, garter belt and stockings—which she put away neatly. After slipping into an elegant satin robe with a bold blue-and-green pattern, she hung up clothing that needed to go into the closet.

After unpacking, she began walking around the room. Studying her surroundings as though she wanted to acquaint herself with the living space, she was really looking for the hidden camera that Alex had warned her might be in the room. She found it in the elaborate molding of a picture frame. Turning away, she had to suppress a shiver as she imagined Madam Dupré and Frank watching her on a monitor and commenting on her figure and her reaction to the room.

It was almost certain that *somebody* was watching her now, because she was the new girl and they wanted to keep tabs on her.

Fighting the impulse to quickly use the equipment Alex had provided to disable the camera, she picked up her makeup case and took it into the bathroom.

"So here I am in this opulent room," she said out loud. "Number eight. It's very grand. I couldn't have asked for anything better."

She was speaking for Alex's benefit, letting him know that she was all right. But she didn't want to overdo it. And she obviously couldn't tell him about the camera. She searched for other electronic equipment in the bathroom. Luckily, it appeared that she'd have privacy in here.

Now that she'd established one-way contact with him, she imagined him picturing her getting ready for her bath as she ran water in the large tub. Trying to ignore the sensation of being observed, she filled the tub, then added scented salts and treated herself to a luxurious soak before dressing in a comfortable outfit that wasn't too flashy.

She was too nervous to eat much, but she figured she'd better get something into her stomach, so she headed for the kitchen.

It was large and well equipped, because it also provided meals for the club. Two uniformed cooks were preparing food and several women were sitting around a banquet-size table along one wall. The cooks glanced up briefly and went back to work. The women studied her with interest, and she wondered how she came across in their eyes. Did they welcome her because she represented another warm body to take part of the workload, or did they see her as a rival?

Until now, she hadn't thought too much about the other residents of the house—probably because she had never liked being plunked down into a group of people new to her.

However, she made her voice sound chipper as she said, "Hello, I'm Gillian."

Cindy, Pam, Babs and Dolly all bid her welcome. They all seemed to be in their twenties. All good-looking. Cindy and Dolly were blondes. Pam had brown hair and Babs was a redhead—although she suspected that all of them were playing around with hair coloring products. Babs and Pam were heavily made up. Cindy and Dolly seemed to go for a natural look.

They were eating a meal of chicken salad, cottage cheese and fruit compote, and Gillian took small portions of each, picking at the food while she answered questions about her background, using the script that Alex had given her. For the most part, the women seemed friendly. Like gals she might have met at a health club or some reading group.

Yeah, sure. She couldn't stop herself from picturing them going over to Bourbon Street Libations to pick up drugged patrons.

How did that work, exactly? Did Jack drug a mark, then give the madam a call? Or did some of the women hang around there? Certainly that wouldn't be the new girl's job. They'd want to be sure of her before she got that kind of assignment. Or would that be part of her initiation, like stripping for the madam.

Before they could get very far into the introductions, Madam Dupré herself stepped into the room. There was an immediate drop in the conversation, which picked up again as Dolly asked a faltering question about Gillian's favorite television shows.

She scrambled for an answer, drawing a blank at first—then thinking to say that she liked most anything on the style channel—which drew agreement from around the table. And some comments about the gay male decorators and their stylists who were on some of the shows. Pam told her that the TV room was in the basement, along with the gym.

The chatter became less frantic when the madam left the vicinity, leading Gillian to the conclusion that their employer made everyone nervous.

Around quarter to six, most of the women stood up. Gillian did, too. They'd be getting to work soon, she thought with a burst of panic.

"Do you want me to show you around?" Pam offered.

"I'd appreciate it."

The brunette led her to the doorway of the dining room where some members of the club were already eating dinner and then into the parlor where they would meet customers. As they stepped back into the hall, she gave Gillian an appraising look, then murmured, "I can tell you're nervous. Just go with the flow."

"Um," Gillian answered, then added, "Thanks for the reassurance, but I don't want to mess up on this job."

"You'll do fine," the other woman assured her. "You've got the looks and the figure for it. And the experience, I gather. Just be willing to accommodate the customers the way you've learned to do, and you'll be a big success," Pam answered.

Oh great, Gillian thought. The last part was going to be a real problem.

"Do you ever have any trouble?" she whispered. "I mean, with the johns."

"This is an expensive place. So most of the guys here are very refined, you know. Once in a while, somebody gets drunk. But Frank takes care of him."

Gillian thought about that for a moment. "How does he know there's a problem?"

"There's a panic button to the right of your headboard. Didn't anyone show it to you?"

"No. Thanks for the tip," Gillian answered with sincerity.

Back in her room she checked out the call device and was relieved to find it where Pam had said it would be. Then she filled some of the time by taking her special vitamin, almost dropping the caplet in the sink as she fumbled with the bottle.

"Smooth, Seymour," she muttered, then remembered that Seymour wasn't supposed to be her name. Probably Alex had registered the slip. Damn him. It was bad enough trying to keep up this charade without knowing he was listening to every sound she made.

Biting back a groan, she grabbed her makeup case and painted some color onto her pale face, working slowly and carefully. Next, she turned on the special piece of equipment that would jam the signal from the camera in her room. At least it was supposed to work that way. She couldn't be sure. All she could do was hope that the surveillance was disabled. If not, she was in deep kimchi.

Trying to keep her mind in neutral, she dressed carefully in underwear that she'd purchased just for this assignment. It looked sexy, but you really couldn't see through it, she told herself as she turned first one way and then the other, watching the grim-faced woman in the mirror. Next, she selected a silky green wrap dress with a ruffled, low-cut neckline. At seven she slipped on her shoes and murmured, "Time to go down to the parlor and meet our guests."

When she reached the bottom of the stairs, Frank was just opening the front door for two men in business suits. And in the parlor, several of the girls were already chatting with more guests as though they were at an elegant cocktail party. On the surface, it made a very pretty picture, Gillian thought, struggling to view the scene like a disinterested observer.

Madam Dupré was standing by the mantelpiece, talking to a distinguished-looking white-haired man in a navy-blue blazer and gray slacks. With his subtle pin-striped tie and crisp white shirt, he looked as though he was going to attend a business meeting as soon as he concluded his business at this whorehouse.

When the madam gestured for her to join the conversation, she crossed the room, glad that she could stay on her feet without swaying.

"I was telling Jimmy about you. And he expressed an interest in meeting you."

Jimmy No Last Name. Well, what had she expected? That on her first night she'd be handed evidence of exactly which prominent men were patronizing this establishment? And who was interested in drugs along with sexual favors.

"How nice." Gillian gave the man a brilliant smile, making the assumption that he was an important customer. He looked like he was in his fifties, with a ruddy complexion and clear blue eyes. And his blazer and slacks appeared to be custom-tailored.

"I understand you're new here," he said, inspecting her face and figure with frank interest, making her heart start to pound.

"Yes. I'm so lucky to have been offered a place with Madam Dupré," she answered.

The madam acknowledged the comment with a nod.

"Can I get you a drink?" Jimmy asked, and she was thankful that he wasn't going to rush her right upstairs.

"I'd love some white wine."

She walked with him to the bar and waited while another tuxedoed servant fixed the drinks. Hers was weak, she noted. But she wasn't surprised. They chatted for a few minutes, but her brain was so paralyzed that she could only answer automatically. Then Jimmy was asking if she'd like to go upstairs and she managed not to choke on the swallow of wine in her mouth.

Dredging up a smile, she answered, "Yes." As she turned and led him across the room again, her heart was banging so hard inside her chest, she hoped it wasn't making the front of her dress flutter.

She had the feeling that all conversation in the room had stopped, that all eyes were turned on her. That was nonsense, she told herself. Yet she knew that some of the women and Madam Dupré were noting her exit.

Conscious of the man who walked close behind her, she led the way to the room she'd vacated only minutes earlier. The last time she'd looked, it had seemed spacious.

When she closed the door now, it felt like a prison cell. Only, the appointments were a lot more luxurious.

The man who had been introduced as Jimmy took off his jacket and draped it over the back of a chair, then started loosening his tie.

Gillian cleared her throat. "Are you visiting the city?" she asked, hearing the breathy quality of her own voice.

"I'm here frequently. I like to relax at the McDonough Club."

"Oh," she answered, wondering what he'd say if she informed him that this posh club was the center of a drug distribution ring. Of course, for all she knew, he was one of the men who had financed the latest shipment.

"I like your aftershave," she said, instantly thinking how stupid that must sound.

"Thank you." He gave her a direct look. "Why don't you get comfortable? I'd like to see you without that dress."

Well, that was pretty direct, she thought as she fumbled with the tie that held the front panels together, glad that she didn't have to contend with buttons.

Striving for a calm she didn't feel, she laid the dress over the arm of a chair, then turned back to face her customer. She was as covered up as she'd be in a bikini swimsuit, she told herself, yet the way his eyes roved over her body made goose bumps rise on her arms.

He was unbuttoning his shirt, which he tossed on top of her dress. For an old guy, he didn't look half bad, she thought with a kind of strange detachment. Probably he worked out at some athletic club. Or maybe he had a personal trainer.

"You do keep yourself in good shape," she said.

"I try."

She turned to pull back the coverlet, then stared in fascination at the expanse of white sheet she'd exposed. Finding her voice again, she said, "I like to start with a sensuous massage, to get you nice and relaxed."

"That's an interesting touch."

"I hope you'll like it. I'm very skilled with my fingers."

When he chuckled appreciatively, she reached for the jar of cream she'd left on the dresser.

IN THE VAN around the corner, Alex sat with every muscle in his body rigid as he listened to the conversation in Gillian's room. She'd been gone for about twenty minutes. Now she was back—with a guy obviously primed for action. A guy who must have zeroed in on her with the speed of a hawk diving at a rabbit.

It took every ounce of discipline he possessed not to jump out of the van and head for the McDonough Club.

He pictured himself bursting into the room, shouting, "You're under arrest."

Yeah, sure. Instead he was doomed to sit and listen to the sexually explicit conversation between Gillian and a guy who got his jollies at a bordello.

He clenched and unclenched his teeth. She seemed to be handling herself—and the john. She was going to use the cream. And it sure as hell better work. Until it did, he was going to have trouble breathing.

He listened to the sound of bed springs creaking, unable to keep vivid pictures from flashing in his head.

After several long seconds of silence, the guy murmured, "Um, that feels nice."

"Good. You just relax and let me take care of you," she answered in a honeyed voice.

"I've never had a girl do this for me."

"Well, it's my special treatment."

Again there was no dialogue for several moments. Then

he heard Gillian's voice murmuring, "That's right. Just relax. That feels wonderful, doesn't it?"

The guy said something. But his face must have been pressed to the sheets, drowning his answer.

Alex waited with his pulse pounding in his ears for what would happen next.

"How are you?" Gillian questioned, and Alex pressed his hand to the headset so he could hear better.

The guy didn't answer.

"Jimmy, are you sleeping? Well you just enjoy a nice relaxing nap. And I'll wake you up in a little while and tell you what a wonderful time we had together."

"Thank God," Alex muttered, then turned to see Rich watching him with unnerving intensity.

"She's safe for the moment," the other agent said, pretending not to notice that his partner was wound tight as a spring.

"Yeah."

"The only way we can find out how the drug is connected to that place is to have her in there. We need to know how the house is tied into the distribution network."

"Yeah," he answered again, because he knew it was true.

GILLIAN LOOKED AT THE MAN lying on the bed. She wanted to give a shout of triumph. The guy was sleeping. Which gave her about a thirty-minute grace period.

The feeling of elation evaporated like stale smoke when she thought about the camera that she'd discovered earlier. Involuntarily she glanced toward the picture frame where the snooping device was hidden—then cursed herself for an inept fool. If the blasted thing was back on, then she'd just given too much away. Damn. She'd been so pleased with herself.

Tension coursed through her body as she waited for the door to burst open and Madam Dupré and Frank to come pelting into the room to ask what the hell was going on. She knew the madam was interested in her performance. She knew the woman would be watching to see what happened up here.

If the camera was functioning, she'd know exactly what her new girl had done. And now she was going to be questioned. Then they'd decide what to do with her. And she knew it wasn't going to be pretty.

But as the seconds ticked by and nothing happened, Gillian felt her heart rate begin to slow a little.

Easing off the bed, she crossed to the sink where she took a quick swallow of water to moisten her dry mouth. Then she strode to the chair where Jimmy had hung his jacket. Stifling the impulse to glance over her shoulder, she began to check his pockets. The cards in his wallet gave her a great deal of information.

"So, you're James Paxton," she murmured. "And you're the vice president of the Gulf Shores consortium in Lafayette. Does the consortium sell drugs? Or are you strictly legit?"

She pictured the men in the van writing down the information and grinned to herself.

But when she saw the photos of Paxton's wife, children and grandchildren in the wallet, she couldn't help sucking in a sharp breath. The man was married. With a large family. But still he felt the need to come here. She wanted to give him a lecture on family values.

Suddenly she couldn't help wondering if her own father had ever done something like this. Impossible, she told herself. He loved his wife and children. Besides, his job before he'd retired had been in a grocery store. Even after he'd worked his way up to manager of the produce department, there hadn't been much money left over for entertainment. Particularly sordid entertainment.

Ruthlessly she cut off the thoughts of her own family and continued poking through James Paxton's effects, looking for any information that would interest the task force.

CYNTHIA DUPRÉ ENTERED her office, then crossed the Oriental rug to the bookcase and pressed a button that opened a set of locked doors. Behind them were six television screens. Next she sat down at the desk and accessed a control panel where she turned on the monitors—all of which showed a view of one of the upstairs bedrooms.

There was a hidden camera in each, and recording equipment, so she could keep track of the action in all of the chambers.

At the present, she saw scenes of various girls with paying customers.

But there was only one who interested her right now. Gillian Stanwick.

When she pressed the button to activate that camera, the screen flickered for a moment, then went blank.

Cynthia uttered a very unladylike oath. She needed to know how the new girl was performing. And the damn camera was acting up. Eyes narrowed, she fiddled with the controls again. But the results were just as unsatisfactory. Well, she'd have to use other means to find out how Miss Stanwick was doing.

HALF AN HOUR LATER, Alex heard Gillian's voice again and his nerves jumped.

"Jimmy, you were so great in bed. The best man I've had in years. You may be past fifty, but you can still do a girl a world of good. And you were so big and so hard. I can't imagine anyone better equipped to nail a prostitute in a bordello.''

Rich laughed. Alex joined in as they listened to more praise from Gillian on how well the guy had done while in reality most of his time in her bed had been spent sleeping.

Then they could hear the guy mumble a slurred response.

"You were fantastic." Gillian repeated what she'd told him earlier. "I hope you enjoyed being with me."

"Very much," he answered, sounding more awake. "I'll be sure to look for you again the next time I'm in the city."

"Thank you."

Again there were rustling sounds, more incidental conversation, then the room was silent.

"You go on down. I'll just get dressed and straighten the bedroom. I'll be along soon."

The door closed. Then Gillian murmured, "One down. And how many more to go?"

Alex didn't know whether to sigh in relief or to clench his fists. And when the door closed again, he sat with his chest constricted, wondering how much more of this he could take.

Finally he decided that he couldn't just sit here. He had to know if she was really all right.

WHEN GILLIAN ENTERED the parlor where several couples stood around talking, she found Madam Dupré staring in her direction. "I was just about to ask Jimmy how things went," she said, an edge in her voice.

Gillian felt alarm leap in her breast. She'd hoped she'd disabled the camera so nobody could see what had gone on in the room. Or had the madam somehow gotten the equipment working again?

Jimmy joined them.

"How was our new girl?" Madam Dupré asked, her tone more moderate when she addressed her customer.

"She was fantastic. One of the best little ladies I've ever been with. You can be sure I'll ask for her again next time I come to the city."

The madam visibly relaxed and Gillian's own tension came down a notch—until a few minutes later when she looked up and saw the man standing in the doorway.

IT WAS ALEX, wearing a mustache and a blond wig that fit him like his own hair. He was also wearing a business suit, an outfit that was completely outside her experience with the man. She struggled to keep her jaw from dropping. Even with the disguise, she would have known him anywhere. And she couldn't believe his audacity. But he seemed to have the right credentials to prove his club membership, because Frank ushered him into the parlor.

The madam was busy with another customer. When Alex crossed the room, Gillian could only stare at him. Earlier in the evening, she'd felt comfortable in the silk wrap dress. Suddenly she was conscious of how it clung to her breasts and hips.

As if his mind was following the same track as hers, he looked her up and down.

"You must be new here," he said.

"I could say the same for you," she retorted.

He didn't bother with any more small talk, but cut right to the chase. "Let's go upstairs," he said in a gruff voice.

"You make up your mind quickly."

"Maybe I've been on a freighter for six months and I'll self-destruct if I don't have a woman."

"Unlikely," she quipped.

But he was already leading her to the steps and straight to Room Eight.

The minute the door was closed, she whirled to confront him and saw him with the lipstick tube in his hand. As she watched, he twisted the microphone off.

"Are you all right?" he asked, the urgency in his voice tearing at her. She'd held herself together while she'd been here with Jimmy. She'd done everything she was supposed to do. She'd proved that she could handle this assignment.

Now that she was alone in the bedroom with Alex, she felt all the starch go out of her body. When she swayed on flower-stem legs, he surged forward and caught her in his arms, pulling her against him.

And she was helpless to do anything but cling. To her chagrin, she felt tears sting the backs of her eyes and she fought to hold them back.

His hands played with her hair, soothed over shoulders that she couldn't keep from shaking.

"I hated listening to that," he said darkly.

"You think I handled it wrong?" she asked.

"You handled it just right. If you hadn't, I'd make them pull you out of here."

She jerked herself away from him, stood on her own two feet. "No!"

"He was a pretty agreeable guy. The next one could be harder to put to sleep."

"I'll figure it out."

"On-the-job training!"

She stiffened. "What's wrong with that?"

"Plenty."

She'd been on the verge of going to pieces. Now she squared her shoulders. "I don't like your attitude."

He was about to answer when Gillian heard a sound. It was the doorknob jiggling. Before she could react, Alex pulled at the tie that held her dress closed, peeled the garment back, then pressed on her shoulders so that she came down on her knees in front of him, with her face wedged against the fly of his slacks as though she were about to perform a very intimate act.

Chapter Seven

The door opened slowly and Wilma, the maid, stepped into the room. As soon as she spotted the two people in the middle of the rug, she made a strangled sound and stopped short.

From Gillian's position on the floor, she couldn't see the woman's face. But she was sure it registered shock at the picture she and Alex made—him standing and her kneeling in front of him looking like she was deep into her work.

"Oh! I beg your pardon," Wilma gasped. "I…I'm so sorry."

Alex kept a hand on Gillian's shoulder as he turned to face the intruder. "This is a private room. What exactly are you doing here?" he asked in a steely voice.

"I…I beg your pardon," Wilma stammered again. "Madam Dupré said the room was empty. I came up here to…to straighten up while Miss Stanwick was out."

'Well, she's not out. She's busy."

"Yes. I see. I'm so sorry."

The woman backed out the door, closing it firmly behind her. As Alex moved away from Gillian, she wavered on her knees.

With a curse, he strode across the rug and turned the lock, the decisive click ringing in the room.

Gillian scrambled to her feet. As she stood up unsteadily, she realized her dress was gaping open. Quickly she pulled the two front panels back into place and fumbled with the tie.

When she saw that Alex was watching her, she flushed. He waited until the dress was closed, then crossed back to her and cupped his hands over her shoulders, stroking her through the silky fabric of her dress.

"Sorry about the drastic tactics. But I didn't know who was coming through that door. And I wanted to stop them in their tracks."

She swallowed. "Well, the tactic was effective."

"Yeah. Are you okay?" he asked.

"Yes," she forced herself to say.

She hated leaning against him, but she was too unsteady to pull away. When he brought his mouth to her ear, his false mustache tickled her skin. But she ignored the tingly sensation as he asked, "What the hell is going on? Surprise visits by the maid can't be good for business."

Gillian turned her own mouth so that she could speak in a voice barely above a whisper. "Before I went downstairs, I zapped the surveillance camera, using that piece of equipment you gave me. I'm sure the madam was frustrated when she couldn't watch me with my first customer. So she sent poor Wilma—the maid—up to see what was happening up here."

"You know Wilma?"

"I met her when I came back with my luggage."

"And?"

"She seemed nice enough. But I can't be sure her only job is keeping the premises clean. She could be paid to rat on us, for all I know."

Alex nodded and she found herself gripping his arms. Before she'd cloistered herself in the McDonough Club, he'd gone out of his way to warn her that stepping into this assignment would be dangerous. She'd resented the interference. And she'd thought she understood the risks.

Now she knew there were factors she hadn't considered. She could trust no one here. Not the other prostitutes. Not the madam or the butler. And not even the woman who was supposed to clean the rooms.

She lowered her head, hating for Alex to see her sudden show of weakness. But he crooked a finger under her chin and tipped her head up, forcing her to meet his eyes.

"I'm sorry," he whispered.

"For what?"

"For what you're going through."

"Not your fault," she reassured him.

"You should get a bonus from Lieutenant LeBarron when this assignment is over," he said. He continued to look at her. "I can see why you were an instant success down in the parlor. You look stunning."

She might have taken that the wrong way, but the way the color in his eyes deepened told her the comment came from some private place inside him.

She felt his hands slide across her back and into her hair. When he brought her mouth to his, there was no thought of resisting.

As his lips came down on hers, she made a small sound. She was startled again by the unfamiliar mustache. But that was only a small part of the sensations coursing through her.

She had tried her best to stay distant from him. Now she might have worried about giving too much away. But he had let her see some of his own vulnerability. That and her own need wiped any thought of reluctance from her mind.

His mouth moved over her, hungry and aggressive. And

she found herself responding to the essence of him on some deep, primitive level that she barely understood.

Heat sparked between them, like lightning striking dry tinder, burning away all thought but one: she must get as close as she could to this man.

"Yes," he rasped, that single frantic syllable sending bursts of raw sexual energy to all her nerve endings.

When the maid had backed out of the room, Gillian had hastily refastened her dress. Now, when she felt Alex's hands on the tie, she helped him open it again, exposing the front of her to his hot gaze, to his touch.

The hungry way he looked at her sent urgent messages to all the sensitive places of her body. With a frantic motion, he swept the dress off her shoulders. And she just as frantically pulled her arms through the sleeves.

"Did Jimmy see you in that sexy underwear?" he rasped.

"Yes."

He cursed.

She said quickly, "You can't see anything important."

"Clever of you." He laughed, then sobered again. "Not unless you're turned on," he added as he focused on the hard points of her nipples poking through the translucent fabric of her bra. Slowly he raised his hand and she waited with her breath frozen in her lungs for his touch. When he stroked his fingers across the aching tips, she moaned with the pleasure of it.

Again he drew out the anticipation as he carefully pushed the cups down and out of the way, anchoring them below her breasts, exposing her creamy flesh.

He made a strangled exclamation. Then, as if in slow motion, he bent his head, capturing one taut peak in his mouth while he used his thumb and finger on the other one, sending a flood of arousal downward through her body. At that moment she knew that she wanted him, needed him more than she had ever needed a man in her life.

He had invaded this place of danger. He had taken her in his arms. And he had made her forget about everything and everybody but him.

She was grateful for that. But she wanted more from him. She wanted everything he was willing to give her. With no conscious thought on her part, one of her hands slid down to his hips, so that she could anchor herself to him. She felt his erection and moved against it, hearing the low, approving sound in his throat. But that hard shaft was pressed to her stomach and she craved more intimate contact.

It seemed that he did, too. When he backed her toward the bed, there was no thought of refusing. As they came down together on the mattress, she moved so that she had him where she wanted him, pressed to her throbbing center.

He was still dressed, and his clothing was in her way. But she couldn't break the contact. Not yet. So they rocked together, touching and kissing, silently exchanging a world of emotions that neither one seemed to be able to express in words. She wanted this man, and he had come here to tell her the same thing. That was enough for the moment.

He dipped his head, rubbing his face against her breasts, and she gasped with the pleasure of that intimate touch.

Anxious to lie flat on the bed so that Alex could lever on top of her, she reached to pull a pillow out of the way and a wave of scent came toward her.

A man's aftershave.

Not Alex's. Another man who had been in her bed less than an hour earlier. Jimmy.

Nothing had really happened. Nothing that meant anything to either one of them. She had fooled him into thinking she had done much more than massage her special amnesiac cream into his neck and back. Yet the memory of that episode was like a dash of cold water in her face.

When she pushed against Alex's shoulder, he didn't immediately respond.

"Alex, no."

He lifted his head, his eyes coming into focus.

"I can smell him," she said in a broken voice. "I'm so sorry, but I can smell him."

"Who?"

"The guy who was here. You know—not that long ago."

"Yeah." He pushed himself up. When he stared down at her, she wrestled the cups of her bra back into place as she fought not to let the tears break through.

Alex's hand was only inches from her hip, but he didn't touch her. That was good, because if he did, she knew she would break down.

He cleared his throat. "I came in to find out if you were okay."

"Yes."

He climbed off the bed, and she wanted to pull him back, but she kept her hands away from him as she sat up.

"We should talk business. Sorry about that little charade with the maid. Are you feeling better now?" he asked, as he pulled out her lipstick again and turned on the microphone once more.

Hardening her expression, she cleared her throat. "I'm fine now," she answered.

"Good."

"What have you found out that we didn't know before you came?"

Part of her hated the cool tone of his voice, but the sensible part was grateful.

"I've only been here a few hours," she answered.

"Yeah. I realize that."

"I know that the women who work here are afraid of Madam Dupré. I know that Frank, the doorman, provides the muscle. I know that…uh—anesthetic cream—works. I already gave you what I could on Jimmy. Apparently he's a legitimate businessman from Lafayette." She made a small sound. "Well, I guess if he were working for the mob or was a drug dealer, he wouldn't carry their membership cards in his wallet."

"Yeah," he said again.

"And there's something else the police should pursue. I saw some girls here who look young. I think they might be underage. You could use them to close this place down."

Alex shook his head. "We can't close it down until we figure out the drug connection."

"Right," she answered in a small voice. She was jumping the gun, probably because she wanted a way out for herself. But she wasn't going to ask for any special favors.

They were both silent for several moments. "I can tell you that the equipment is working on our end," he said.

"Good," she answered, relieved yet hating the implications.

Alex straightened his clothing. "I'll tell the madam you did a fantastic job," he said.

Before she could answer, he straightened his clothing, then turned and left the room, and the tears that she'd been holding back began leaking from her eyes and down her cheeks. But she crammed her fist against her mouth, making sure that no sound escaped from her throat, because she was damned if she was going to let the guy at the microphone know she was crying.

NEW ORLEANS was a wicked, wicked city. A hothouse where tourists walked around until two in the morning with alcoholic drinks in plastic cups. One famous strip club advertised its wares with a naked woman swinging over the doorway. Bordellos operated with the silent cooperation of the police. Any illegal drug you wanted was easily available on many street corners.

Ricardo Gonzalez had sent a group of his most trusted hombres on ahead to this hotbed of sin. Now he had come from his country, Nilia, to join them, and he was enjoying all of the pleasures of the Crescent City. But he hadn't come simply for a vacation. He had business to conduct—business vital to his success in Nilia.

To that end, he was about to have an important meeting with one of the city's most respected entrepreneurs, Jerome Senegal. Not in one of the city's plush offices. Or even in a hotel suite. He'd wanted more privacy. And Pedro, his most trusted lieutenant, had found the perfect location—a warehouse at the edge of the French Quarter where several of what were called "crews" stored the displays from their Mardi Gras floats.

So now he stood in the shadow of a fifteen-foot-tall statue of the Greek god Neptune. The statue was holding a trident, his presumably massive genitals hidden by a spray of waves.

Ricardo was wishing he could get out of his bulletproof vest when he heard footsteps echoing on the cement floor. Looking to his right, he saw Pedro striding quickly through a side door. "They're coming, *jeffe*."

"Bueno," he answered with absolute confidence. He might have been worried about the security of this meeting place. But he had four of his best men on the catwalk above the main floor. And more were stationed behind other stored items, ready to make sure that the meeting went the way he planned. Even when you dealt with legitimate businessmen, you had to watch your back.

Still, his stomach muscles knotted as Senegal strode into the room, flanked by a human fortress of tough-looking men dressed in dark suits.

They all looked as though they were going to a meeting in a corporate office. But Ricardo wasn't fooled. These guys were prepared to protect their boss from the evil interloper from South America.

Senegal himself was fairly short, not more than five eight. With dark hair and leathery skin that gave him a reptilian look. As he inspected the man, Ricardo knew he was facing someone who was as tough and ruthless as himself, even if the man kept his reputation squeaky clean.

"So, it's good to finally meet," Senegal said.

"Yes," Ricardo answered.

They talked about their business deal for several moments, and Ricardo didn't like the vibes he was picking up. He was used to controlling situations—and he felt control slipping out of his hands.

"I assume there's no problem," he said, his voice tight.

Senegal stood his ground, but his words weren't exactly reassuring. "There's been a little glitch," he murmured.

"Oh?"

"We'll work it out."

So what was the problem? Didn't this guy have the merchandise he'd pledged? Was that the reason for the sudden reluctance? Or did he have cold feet?

"I hope we *can* work it out," Ricardo said carefully. "Because it will go very hard with you if you back out of the deal."

Senegal stared coldly at him, using a look that Ricardo recognized, because it was an important fixture in his own repertoire. "Are you threatening me on my own turf?"

Ricardo answered with a small shrug.

"Who the hell do you think you are, amigo? This is my city. I make the rules here."

Keeping his own voice calm, Ricardo stated the facts. "It doesn't matter what city we're in. I'm telling you that when a man makes a deal with me, he keeps his promise."

Senegal slipped his hand into his pocket. Apparently that was the signal for two of his aides to draw the guns hidden under their suit jackets.

Ricardo's hombres responded instantly, stepping from the shadows, their weapons drawn.

At that moment there was so much tension in the room that Ricardo imagined he could see lightning crackling on the Mardi Gras paraphernalia. His men would save him, he knew. But the carnage would be great. Some of them would die in this warehouse. And more of the opposition would go down.

Then Senegal cleared his throat. "There's no need for violence. We don't want anyone to get hurt here."

"I agree."

"We both have the same goal. We should be friends."

"Yes," Ricardo replied.

"Put your weapons away," the local man said to his men.

Senegal's guards instantly obeyed.

Ricardo gave a similar order and the tension in the room ratcheted down several notches.

"The deal will work out," Senegal said. "And as a gesture of my good will, and a show of good faith, I'd like to extend an invitation to a special private party with some exquisite young ladies."

"Thank you," Ricardo answered.

The deal better work out, he thought. Or Senegal was a dead man. But meanwhile, he would accept the businessman's hospitality.

ONCE AGAIN, ALEX WOKE before the alarm went off. This time he was dreaming of Gillian—in his bed.

His eyes blinked open and he turned his head, almost expecting to see her snuggled next to him under the covers. Which was crazy. He'd never brought a woman here to this house. It was his private sanctuary. The little world he'd created for himself, where nobody would ever make it clear he was in the way. Nobody would lock the door when they were angry with him. Nobody would dress him in thrift shop clothing so that the other kids at school had a field day teasing him. And nobody would tell him to open a can of beans for dinner.

He centered himself here and went out to face the world. This house had helped save his sanity in those last wretched months with the P.D.

But Gillian was invading his space, whether he liked it or not. He'd been on the verge of making love with her the night before. Then she'd stopped him, and both of them had realized that was for the best.

He'd steered them back to a business discussion and both of them had regained their cool. But he wasn't feeling cool now. And he damn well hoped she wasn't, either.

"No," he said aloud. "Don't be a jerk. She's in a hell of a situation, and she has to focus on her assignment—not on you."

GILLIAN WOKE in her opulent bedroom. For a moment she didn't know where she was because she'd never slept in a place this plush. Then it all came flooding back and she squeezed her eyes closed again.

But she knew it was impossible to hide behind her closed lids. With a sigh, she opened her eyes. From the sunshine filtering in around the edges of the curtains, she judged that it must be late in the morning. At least nobody had come in to wake her up early. She didn't have to be out on patrol today. She didn't have anything to do until this evening when she'd have to bring men up here again and pretend to service them.

She wanted to cancel that last thought. As she looked around the room, it was almost possible to convince herself that she was in a luxury bed-and-breakfast. The furniture, the wall coverings and the window treatments were certainly right. But the expensive ambience couldn't dispel the atmosphere of menace that hovered in the room. This place might be beautiful. But it was evil. And she was part of that evil as long as she stayed here.

She was here only temporarily, Gillian told herself firmly. She might not like what she was doing. But she was in this room for an important reason—to bring down a drug and prostitution ring. And the ends would justify the means.

She had to believe that, or she couldn't go on with the role she'd been assigned.

But what would happen when the police cracked the case? Would her name get into the papers? Would her family find out what she'd been doing?

She took her lower lip between her teeth as she pictured the reaction of Mom and Dad. They were proud that she'd joined the police force. But they didn't know what she was doing now.

And they'd better not find out. Surely when a cop was working undercover, the papers would keep her name out of the story.

As she lay in the large bed, she tried to make her breathing even. But there were too many reasons for her nerves to be screaming.

It wasn't just the role she'd been assigned or imagining her parents' reaction. Last night when Alex had come rushing into the parlor and brought her upstairs, he'd acted as though he cared about her. Could she trust those feelings? Or had he only been swept along by the whole situation?

And how would he see her when all this was over? She was working undercover for the police department, yet the job wasn't exactly making her feel good about herself. If *she* had trouble coping with the implications, how would a guy react who was listening to every moment of her sordid existence in this room?

There was no way to answer that question. With a grimace, she climbed out of bed and stretched. Her mind told her to forget about a relationship with Alex. But as she stood beside the bed, she couldn't help wondering if he was on duty in the van.

"My first morning in this charming house," she said aloud, wishing he could answer her. "So far, so good."

Then she went into the bathroom, where she took a quick shower, blew her hair dry and dressed in the most conservative outfit she could find—a white silk blouse and navy silk slacks.

"See you later," she said to the room before going down to the kitchen.

IN THE SURVEILLANCE VAN, Alex scowled at the recording equipment and pressed his lips together.

"Nice of her to tell us she's leaving the room," Seth Lewis observed.

Alex's usual partner was Rich Stewart. But Seth was working with him that morning because he'd asked to do a couple of surveillance shifts so he'd get a better picture of the whole assignment.

It was extra duty for the agent, and Alex gave him credit for that. In truth, there were pluses and minuses to the temporary arrangement. He'd sent Seth out to bring them coffee from one of the shops in the French Quarter. On the other hand, he didn't like having a new guy here, seeing how uptight he was about Gillian.

"So, can you track her around the house?" Seth asked.

"Not unless she carried her lipstick with her, which would look a little strange. We don't want anyone taking a close look at it."

"So you don't know if she gets into trouble."

"No," Alex snapped without looking at Seth, feeling like that one syllable had given too much away.

His suspicions were confirmed by the other agent's next question. "Did you know her from the police department?"

"She wasn't on the force when I was there," Alex answered evasively, keeping his voice neutral, hoping to cut the conversation short.

Apparently, Seth got the message because he stopped probing, then pointed to one of the TV monitors.

"Who's that guy?" he asked, gesturing toward a tall, thin man with greasy hair who was coming down the alley toward the back door of the bordello. He had two scruffy-looking blond girls with him.

"Damned if I know," Alex answered.

"It looks like he's rounded up some street kids," Seth murmured.

"I'd like to warn them what they're getting into."

"Yeah, so would Gillian. She told me something about seeing underage kids," Alex agreed. "But we've all got to stay on task."

Both of them fell silent as they stared at the door where the girls had disappeared.

A DOZEN WOMEN who were sitting around the table in the kitchen looked up as Gillian entered. Some wore attractive robes. Others had put on casual clothing.

"Come sit beside me," Pam said, patting the wooden

chair to her right, then introduced her to the women she hadn't met yet.

Gratefully, Gillian joined her.

"Coffee?" Dolly asked.

"Yes, thanks," she answered as the blonde passed the pot of strong, chicory-laced brew.

She helped herself to a carton of apricot yogurt from a tray in the middle of the table. Other women were eating fruit or scrambled eggs.

The conversation was about the weather, hair and makeup and clothing. Then Pam lowered her voice and made a comment about one of the customers.

"Did you see how much Drew was drinking last night?"

"Yes."

"I guess he must be having problems at work."

"Or with his wife," Lisa supplied, following the statement with a small laugh.

There were murmurs around the table.

Just at that moment, Madam Dupré swept into the room. At the sight of her, the conversation stopped dead, much as it had the afternoon before.

One of the cooks had been approaching the table with a plate of scrambled eggs. He stepped quickly back, out of the line of fire, it seemed.

The madam gave Lisa a pointed look, and the woman's face turned pale.

"Were you discussing one of our patrons?" the madam asked in a voice edged with ice.

"I, uh," the unfortunate woman stammered as she sank lower into her chair.

Madam Dupré folded her arms across her chest. "You know that making negative comments about our patrons is against the rules."

"Yes, ma'am."

"To help you remember, I will be deducting twenty per cent from your earnings for the week."

"Yes, ma'am," Lisa answered meekly.

Pam looked down at her plate but didn't volunteer that she should also have her wages docked, since she was the one who had started the conversation.

"How are you doing this morning?" the madam asked, her tone switching abruptly from icy to sweet, and Gillian realized she was the subject of the question.

"Fine," she answered.

"I'm glad to hear it. We're one big happy family here. And I'm sure you'll fit right in."

"I'm sure," Gillian murmured, thinking that if she fulfilled her assignment, she'd be breaking up the happy family. What would happen to these women? How would they make a living? She hoped her thoughts weren't showing on her face as she spooned up some yogurt.

The madam poured herself a mug of coffee and left the room. It was several moments before the conversation picked up again.

Some of the residents of the house got up and quickly exited. Others lingered over breakfast. Gillian stayed to pick up as much information as she could. Fifteen minutes later, another door from the hall opened and a man strode into the kitchen.

He was tall and skinny, about forty she judged, with greasy dark hair that made Gillian want to wipe her fingers on her napkin.

He looked around the table and zeroed in on her immediately. Walking closer to her, he asked, "Who are you?"

Setting down her cup with a clatter, she said, "Gillian Stanwick." She wished she'd been able to wipe the quaver from her voice.

"I wasn't informed that we had a new girl," he said brusquely. "How long have you been here?"

"Madam Dupré hired me yesterday."

"Is that right?" He gave her one more long look, then strode out of the room.

When his footsteps had receded, she looked toward Pam. "Who is he?"

Pam spoke in a low voice. "Maurice Gaspard. He's the owner, you know."

"I thought that was Madam Dupré."

"She works for him. Or maybe they're partners. But he's definitely in charge. If you think she can be nasty, watch out for him. I saw him drag—"

Pam stopped talking abruptly when Frank came to the kitchen door and looked at Gillian. "You're wanted in the office," he said.

"Yes," she answered, standing so quickly that her chair vibrated. She knew that everybody still in the kitchen, including the cooks, was looking at her.

Telling herself to stay cool, she followed him down the hall to the office where she'd first been interviewed.

When she knocked, it was Gaspard who called out, "Come in."

Even from where she stood, she didn't like the tone of his voice. But her only choice was to comply.

"Close the door," he said coldly.

Gillian complied, then turned to face the occupants of the room. In the kitchen, there had been no doubt that Madam Dupré was in charge. Now, as she sat behind her own desk, her features were pinched and her hands were clenched around her delicate china mug. The man named Gaspard was sitting in one of the guest chairs, his posture apparently relaxed. But when he swiveled around and turned toward Gillian, she saw that his expression was stormy.

He looked from Gillian to the madam.

"Please explain how this woman ended up under my roof."

"She came with excellent recommendations. Since we had a vacancy, I was happy to get her."

"You know that I expect to be consulted on the hiring of new personnel."

"Yes, but I was sure you would approve. And I took the opportunity to fill out our roster."

"Have you checked her references?" he asked, as though Gillian weren't even in the room.

"Of course," she said quickly. Then added. "I've done an initial check."

"Finish the process," he said, his voice low and very controlled.

"I intend to." The madam cleared her throat. "She entertained two different customers last night. They both gave her excellent ratings. I believe she will be an asset to our business."

Gaspard stroked his pointy chin, then swung his attention back to Gillian. The way he looked her up and down, then focused on her breasts, made her skin crawl. "I hope so," he said in a low, silky voice, then went on, "Maybe I should find out for myself how well she does in bed."

Gillian's mouth had gone dry. There was nothing she could do but stand with her hands pressed to her sides, waiting to hear if he was planning to take her straight upstairs to try her out. And this time, she wouldn't be able to put him to sleep, because her vitamins had long since worn off.

Chapter Eight

"I'm sure she'd be glad to give you a private audition later," Madam Dupré said. "Right now, I believe we have other business. Don't you agree?"

Gillian fought not to let her revulsion show on her face.

He waited long moments before answering, *"Oui."* Then he gave Gillian a dismissive look and said, "Leave us now."

"Yes, sir," she managed, then turned and left the office. Sickness rose in her throat as she stood in the hall outside the office.

Yet she didn't run down the hall. Instead she took a steadying breath, then pressed her ear to the door.

"I was disturbed to learn that another one of those young girls has disappeared," Gaspard said, a dangerous edge in his voice.

"Take that up with Frank," the madam snapped.

"I'd like to hear what *you* have to say about it," Gaspard jeered.

Gillian wanted to hear more. But the sound of a chair scraping made her go pale. If Gaspard came to the door and caught her spying, she hated to think what he might do.

Every cell in her body urged her to run in the other

direction, but she forced herself to walk away calmly. When she turned a bend in the hall, she felt as though she'd escaped her own execution.

Although she'd tried to prepare herself for this assignment, some protective instinct had kept her from conjuring up the image of anyone like Gaspard putting his hands on her. She ached to keep walking toward the back of the house, into the alley and away from this place. But that was not an option. And probably some alarm would go off if she stepped outside.

She squared her shoulders. Chin tipped up, she was heading toward the back stairs when she heard voices coming from one of the other rooms off the hall. A man was talking to Frank. The important client Gaspard had mentioned? She couldn't see either one of the speakers, but the one she didn't recognize had a suave, cultured New Orleanian drawl. Definitely a polished, upper-class accent. But the subject of his conversation didn't sound upper class. When she realized what he was saying, the breath froze in her lungs.

"You have another of the young ones for me?"

"Of course, sir. A very lovely girl. Very young. Very inexperienced, the way you like them."

"A virgin?"

"I can't answer that for sure."

"Yes, I understand. But I want the usual arrangement."

"Of course, sir."

Gillian clenched her jaw. From both conversations she'd just overheard, it sounded like something very nasty was going on in this house. The two men stepped into the hall. For just a second, Gillian caught the profile of the man who had made the special request for a girl young enough to be his daughter. He appeared to be in his mid-fifties; the skin under his chin sagged just a little, and his brown hair had a touch of gray at the temples. There was something familiar about him, but she couldn't say what—not from the one quick look she got before he turned his back and walked in the other direction.

Intent on learning more, Gillian took a step forward. But as she started down the hall, a hand grabbed her arm—stopping her in her tracks.

FEAR ROSE IN HER THROAT and she jerked around expecting to see Gaspard's fierce visage. But it was Pam who had just come from the direction of the kitchen.

"No," she mouthed.

"But…"

The restraining hand tightened on her arm. "Stay out of it," Pam murmured, pulling her into a room that looked like a private lounge.

"What's going on?"

Pam spoke in a low voice. "You heard. It's, you know, one of the guys who comes here because the house can provide him with tender young flesh."

"What guys?"

"Some of them are important men in town. It's better if you don't know too much about it."

"Okay then, what girls?"

When the other woman spoke again, her voice was tight. "You know. Runaways. Kids who come to the city because they have nowhere else to go. Gaspard trolls for them. He makes friends with the pretty ones and offers to find them a place to stay. Some of them fall for it."

"Not any of the women I met at breakfast."

"Well, some of them came from that part of the operation. They've grown up fast and joined our group. We don't have too much contact with the others. They stay in another part of the house."

Gillian looked back over her shoulder at the closed door, trying to imagine that other part of the house, and felt her chest tighten. One of the girls had apparently escaped this morning. But she wasn't going to mention that to Pam since she'd have to admit she'd been eavesdropping. "Grown men, forcing themselves on teenagers. That's…that's immoral."

Pam sighed. "If you were one of those churchgoing busybodies, you could say that everything that happens here is immoral."

"But we came here by choice. Those girls didn't," Gillian answered.

Pam gave her an unsettling look. "I don't know about you, but my choices were limited."

Gillian might have pursued that line of discussion, but the previous one was more pressing. "Is there anything we can do to help those girls?"

Pam gave her a considering look. Then her features firmed. "What—do you want to get in trouble with Gaspard? Or didn't you get enough of him a few minutes ago?"

Gillian nodded, thinking that it would be dangerous to risk another run-in with the man who owned this house. And dangerous to exchange too much information with Pam. As for Gaspard, she hadn't even known about him before she came here. She'd bet that New Orleans Confidential hadn't, either, since Alex had been pretty thorough in his briefings.

"Who is he?" she asked, hoping she could get more information out of Pam. Without giving too much away.

"Like I said, he owns this place. Or—he's working for someone else."

"Who?"

Pam tipped her head to one side, regarding her for several seconds. "If you haven't figured it out for yourself, I'll give you a piece of advice. It's not healthy to ask a bunch of questions. Just do your job and keep your mouth shut."

Gillian felt the hairs on the back of her neck prickle. Last night and this morning, she'd gotten a couple of pointers on the dangers of the McDonough Club. In fact, every moment that she spent here seemed to provide another lesson.

"Thanks for the guidance," she answered, sincerely grateful for the reminder. Lowering her voice, she added what she hoped was an authentic touch, "I've always been on my own, until now. I guess I thought that working in a place like this would be safer. But…"

"Come get another cup of coffee," Pam said, obviously changing the subject. "The coffee here is really good."

"I noticed," Gillian answered, then followed Pam into the now empty kitchen.

"We can sit out on the sunporch. It's almost like being out of our cage," her new friend said. Gillian wrapped her hands around her mug.

"Too bad we don't have some of my mom's blueberry muffins," Gillian said. As soon as the words were out of her mouth, she knew she'd made a mistake.

"Your mom baked muffins?" Pam asked, cocking an eyebrow.

"Uh, yeah."

"Sounds like you came from a warm and fuzzy home."

Gillian wanted to say that she had. Instead, she mumbled, "It was okay—some of the time."

Before they could drink any of the coffee, Dolly came downstairs.

"Where were you?" she asked Pam. "Did you forget you promised to help me with a new hairstyle?"

"Sorry," Pam murmured, setting her own mug down.

"That's okay," Gillian answered. "I'll just stay here awhile before I go up."

She was making her way toward the sunporch as the back door opened and a man came in. She went very still.

IT WAS ALEX—for the second time in ten hours, wearing the brown uniform of a delivery man. But it wasn't his clothing that startled her. Instead of a man in his thirties, he looked about ten years younger. Somehow he'd transformed himself from a hardened cop into a wet-behind-the-ears delivery boy. As she surveyed him assessingly, she decided that the altered look came partly from the way he'd styled his hair. Then there was the makeup that had darkened his skin, the way he walked and the hip sunglasses hiding his eyes.

She could only stare at him—speechless. It appeared that he must have known she was alone in the kitchen and he'd chosen that moment to seek her out again.

"Who...who are you supposed to be?" she stammered, then glanced around, thankful that neither of the cooks was in the vicinity to hear how stupid that must sound.

"I'm the substitute driver from Cajun Perks, in case you didn't know where that brew in your hand came from," he said, his chipper voice matching his appearance. "The regular guy's sick, so I don't know my way around. Where do I put the coffee, *chère*?"

"I'm new here. But as it happens, I can answer that," she said, recovering quickly.

"Just let me get the bags." He opened the back door and brought in a box holding several large bags of coffee. She set down her mug, then picked up some of the bags and led him to the pantry, where they stowed the beans with the other supplies.

Before she could ask what he was doing here, he answered the question.

"I want to have a look at the office," he insisted.

"The office. You don't mean, the madam's office. The last I knew, she was in there with a guy named Maurice Gaspard."

"I saw him out in the alley—on one of the monitors. He had a couple of girls with him. Who is he?" Alex asked.

"At breakfast, they told me he's the owner. Or the senior partner. The madam is afraid of him."

Alex took in her rigid stance. "I'd say you are, too."

She couldn't answer.

His eyes turned fierce as he gripped her by the shoulders. "What did he do to you?"

"Nothing!"

"You're lying."

She swallowed. "He was angry because Madam Dupré hired me without consulting him."

He gave her another long inspection and his words told her he was reading between the lines. "If he steps into your bedroom, I'll be here before he can take two breaths."

She nodded, knowing he was telling the truth and thankful that he'd made the offer. Still, she hoped he wasn't going to come charging into the house like that, because they'd probably both blow their assignments.

ALEX DUG THE NAILS of one hand into his palm, struggling to get control of his emotions. He'd better calm down, because he was in danger of crossing an invisible line. From undercover agent to...what? He wasn't ready to put a label on his feelings. All he knew was that he and Gillian had an assignment to complete and he wasn't going to blow it.

But he'd decided last night that the sooner he got her out

of this house of horrors, the better. Which was why he was back this morning—doing some strategic snooping.

"There's another office near here," he said, keeping his voice even. "We can have a look in there."

"How do you know?" she asked.

"We got some information from a guy who worked at the club before it changed hands. Was there a computer on the madam's desk?"

"I don't think so," she answered.

He nodded in satisfaction. "Then we'll have a go at the alternate location."

She stepped back and let him lead her into the hall, then down a few paces to another door.

"I walked past here several times," she murmured as he turned the knob.

The door was locked and he cursed softly under his breath. But he was prepared for that, too. Pulling a set of picks out of his pocket, he went to work on the lock. When he heard the mechanism click, he made a soft sound of satisfaction.

"Hurry up," Gillian muttered, and he heard the tension in her voice. He'd like to question her some more about what had happened to her that morning, but he'd better not do it now. Pushing the door open, he led her inside, then locked the door behind them. The room was in shadow, and it took several moments for his eyes to adjust. In fact, there was a computer, a printer and a fax machine sitting on a desk.

Crossing to the equipment, he touched the computer keyboard. The screen sprang to life.

As he studied the directory, he saw a list of women's names. Pam, Dolly, Babs, Lisa, Cindy, Amy and half a dozen others.

Gillian leaned over his shoulder and he felt the warmth

of her body radiating to his. "Some of those are the names of the women in the house," she said. "Others I don't recognize. And there's something else I have to tell you. A little while ago, I heard some more about the underage girls here."

"The kids that Gaspard guy was bringing in?" Alex asked.

"Yes. They seem to be held captive in another part of the house. According to Pam."

"Who is she?"

"Another one of the women who works here," Gillian continued. "She says Gaspard makes friends with them on the streets and brings them in. I found out there are slimy guys who like them better in bed than the more experienced women who live upstairs."

"Nice," Alex muttered, his voice dripping with sarcasm.

"One of those men was here a little while ago, requesting a girl."

"Anyone you recognize?"

"Well, there was something familiar about him. But I only caught a glimpse of his face. He looked like he was in his fifties. He looked upper class. And he spoke with a courtly Southern drawl. But he gave me the creeps."

"Yeah."

"What can we do about guys like him coming here?"

"Nothing. Not until we nail down the drug connection."

She answered with a tight nod, and he turned back to the computer. "So some of these names could be those girls. Or former employees."

"What happened to them?" she asked, unable to keep her tone perfectly steady.

He shrugged, keeping his own voice even. "They hit the jackpot and left."

"Sure," she murmured, and the cynical note in her voice

made him want to turn and pull her close. Instead he focused on the computer. "This could be a record of what each of them earns or earned."

"Or it's a code," she suggested. "Maybe it has to do with the drugs, only they're being cagey."

"Yeah." When he tried to click on the Lisa file, he was asked for a password.

"Any idea what that might be?" he asked.

"No."

He tried several possibilities, but he didn't have enough knowledge of the operation or the players to make an educated guess. And he didn't expect Gillian to know much more—not yet.

While he tried to get into the files, she searched the drawers. He gave her credit for not wasting time while she was in the office.

"Here's something interesting," she said.

He clicked back to the previous screen, then turned away from the frustrating session at the computer to look at the leather-bound book she'd pulled from the second drawer on the left.

He flipped through the pages and found notations that consisted of numbers and letters.

"This time, I'm sure it's a code," Gillian muttered.

He nodded his agreement.

"I have no idea what it means," she added quickly.

"We don't have to figure it out in the next five minutes," he told her as he pulled out another piece of equipment that he'd brought—a miniature camera.

"Hold the pages open," he directed as he set the book on the desk.

Remembering the way they'd gotten surprised the night before, he kept one ear peeled toward the hall while he worked.

As Gillian flattened the pages, keeping her hand out of the way so he could photograph the information, he was hoping that there would be someone back at headquarters who could take a stab at the meaning of the numbers and letters. Or maybe they could send it to the National Security Agency. A whorehouse code should be a piece of cake for the spooks at Ft. Meade.

There were a lot of pages in the book.

"Do you want me to keep holding these open, or should I go back to the desk?" Gillian asked.

"The desk," he answered, reaching for a rounded glass paperweight and using it to hold the next page open.

He had just put the book away when someone tried to turn the knob on the door through which they'd entered.

He and Gillian both went still.

"Is someone in there?" a voice called out.

Neither one of them answered the question.

"Go away," Gillian muttered under her breath.

In the hall, footsteps receded. They waited, neither of them moving. Just as they both breathed a sigh of relief, a section of the paneling to Alex's right began to slide slowly open.

He'd promised to keep his hands off Gillian. But that was when he thought they had some privacy. Now he pulled her into his arms and covered her mouth with his.

Giving an excellent picture of a man who was totally absorbed in what he was doing, Alex moved his lips over Gillian's. After a moment of shocked surprise, she responded with equal enthusiasm.

And when he pulled out the tail of her shirt, slipped his hand underneath and flattened his palm against her back, she didn't protest.

He had several heartbeats to wonder if she was just putting on an act before a young woman stepped into the room.

Standing with the panel gaping open behind her, the woman said, "What are you doing here?"

Alex gave her a cocky look that went with the personality he'd put on with his delivery boy uniform. "Looking for some privacy," he said. "What are *you* doing here?"

Ignoring the question, she addressed herself to Gillian. "Don't tell me you're giving the good stuff away. You can get in big trouble if the madam finds out you've got something going on the side."

Gillian took a step away from him and faced the newcomer. "Pam, I hope you won't tell her," she said, her tone properly pleading. "A-Alex and I wanted to…you… know…be alone together."

He kept a protective arm around her shoulder. "So what are *you* doing here?" he asked the newcomer again.

Probably because he'd put her off balance, the woman turned and carefully closed the panel.

"We're all in trouble if somebody catches us," Gillian said softly. "So we should stick together."

The woman named Pam nodded and he hoped to hell they could trust her.

"Why were you willing to risk getting caught sneaking in here?" Gillian probed.

Pam swallowed. "You're not like the usual timid girl who ends up with Madam Dupré, you know."

"No. But neither are you."

The other woman considered that for several moments, then echoed Alex's previous thought. "I guess I have to trust you."

He wasn't going to take that on faith.

"I hope you won't say anything about this," Gillian pressed.

Pam responded with a tight nod. After a moment of silence she said, "I guess you noticed this morning that I got Lisa in trouble."

"Then you kept your head down while she took the heat," Gillian added.

"Right. But I figured I could fix it in the computer so she didn't get any money deducted from her account."

Gillian's eyes widened. "You can do that?" she asked.

"Yes. I used to work with computers—in my old life." Pam moved to the desk and tapped the keyboard. The screen, which had gone black again, leaped to life once more.

"Won't the madam notice?"

"She probably put a notation in the file, but she doesn't keep the accounts. There's a guy who comes in for that, you know."

"What guy?" Alex asked quickly.

She shrugged. "He's a friend of mine."

"Oh yeah? Are you telling me you like living dangerously, too?" Alex asked.

Pam merely glanced over her shoulder at him and gave him a saucy wink before bringing up the screen with the names of the women. She clicked on Lisa's file, confirming that the list really did refer to the women working in the establishment. When she was asked for a password, she typed rapidly on the keyboard.

"How do you know the password?" Alex asked.

"My friend gave it to me, you know."

When she'd brought up Lisa's file, she went in and removed the notation about reducing her earnings.

"So what else is in the computer?"

"I haven't had occasion to find out," she answered, but the little catch in her voice told him that she was probably lying.

"How did you find the secret panel?" he asked.

"We have a lot of spare time during the day. And I like to have a good handle on my environment."

Alex nodded, thinking that was a pretty good policy and also wondering if this woman was more than she seemed to be. He'd like to check on her. But even if he found out her last name, it might be an alias.

Apparently she was anxious to clear out. "Well, I'll leave you two lovebirds alone," she said.

"Show me how the panel works," Gillian said, "so we can get in here whenever we want to."

Pam turned to her inquiringly. "If you didn't use the panel, how did you get in?"

He saw her face go a shade whiter as she realized she'd made a tactical mistake.

He made a split second decision and said, "The door to the hall was unlocked."

"Oh yeah? That's interesting," the prostitute answered. "Don't tell the madam, or Frank will get in trouble. And if he knows you ratted on him, you'll be sorry."

"I wasn't planning to say anything," Gillian answered quickly.

Behind Pam's back, they exchanged a look that said they were both wondering if the woman believed their story.

She turned to the section of the wall and demonstrated the hidden mechanism. Alex stepped through and saw a small passageway that led to the back of a closet where coats were hung.

"The closet opens into a side hall," Pam said.

"Thanks," he answered.

"See you later," the woman said and disappeared.

Alex stepped back into the room.

"Do you think she believes us?" Gillian asked in a low voice.

"I hope so. But we have to stay here for a while to make it look good."

Gillian nodded. "I don't want to take a chance on any more snooping. Not now."

"Okay," he agreed, because his thoughts were similar. They'd had a close call, and he didn't want to put Gillian in an even worse position. But after holding her in his arms a few minutes ago, he couldn't simply stand here staring at her. And he was hoping she felt the same way. When he held out his arms, she came to him and leaned her head against his shoulder.

He stroked his hand over her back, then reached to play with her hair.

"How are you doing?" he asked.

"I've been better. And don't give me any crap about 'I told you so.'"

"I'll keep my mouth shut on that point," Alex murmured.

"What other points do we have to discuss?"

"Well, we don't really know if Pam was telling the truth about what she was doing here. Do you believe the story she told us?"

"I'll reserve judgment on that," Gillian finally answered. "Maybe she's some sort of spy. The question is for whom?"

He shrugged. "Maybe you'll get a handle on that. But more important, do you think she'll turn us in?"

Gillian shook her head. When she tipped her face up toward his, the troubled look in her eyes tore at him. He wanted to wipe the anxiety off her face, but there was nothing he could say to reassure her. The only thing he could do was lower his mouth to hers again for a passionate kiss.

His goal was to make her forget where they were and

why. At least for the moment. Perhaps he wanted to forget that, too.

He didn't have to coax her to open her lips. She did that at once, giving him a taste of her intoxicating essence.

He angled his head first one way and then the other, wanting more of her and still more.

When he finally had to draw a breath, she whispered his name and he raised his face to look at her—seeing her skin so white in the dim light.

One of her hands lifted, slowly, slowly to touch his face. "Thank you for being here," she whispered.

There wasn't much he could do for her. Not on a twenty-four-hour basis. She was locked in this house of horrors and all he could manage was a couple of brief appearances.

The realization brought a desperate edge to his emotions as he found her mouth again. Gathering her close, he absorbed the feel of her body against his.

It wasn't enough. Not hardly. Shifting her upper body, he slid his hand between them so that he could cup one of her breasts.

Her blouse was thin. So was her bra, and he could feel the tight crest of her nipple pressing against his palm.

The potent combination of his mouth on hers and his hand on her breast fueled the buzz that had started in his head.

When she murmured something incoherent, he deepened the kiss. Hot need flowed through his body. Leaning back against the desk, he gathered her in, rocking her hips against his as he devoured her mouth, using his tongue, his lips, his teeth in an assault that should have gotten him arrested.

Her lower body moved urgently against his.

For long moments nothing existed in the universe besides the two of them giving and taking pleasure with each other.

Every reaction, every nuance, ricocheting through him, each sensation reinforcing the others until his senses were swamped.

Then sanity came zinging back. He was going out to the van when he left this room. Seth would expect a report. And he wanted to be able to explain what had happened in this room with a straight face.

So he lifted his mouth from Gillian's. "Honey," he breathed, "I'm afraid we have to get out of here before somebody else discovers us."

He watched her vision come back into focus, watched the expression on her face go from spaced-out to practical—with a touch of something that made his chest tighten.

"Yes," she murmured, reaching to tuck in her blouse. She took several deep breaths, then said, "Why don't I try that hidden door—to make sure I know how it works."

Before he could answer, she swept out of the room, and he knew that he'd hurt her by stopping things so abruptly. But maybe that was good. Maybe the two of them could keep this impersonal.

Sure. Right.

GILLIAN CLOSED THE CLOSET door firmly but quietly behind her, stepped into the side hall and gave herself several minutes to get her breathing under control. When she felt nearly back to normal, she checked her face in a nearby mirror. Satisfied with her appearance, she scanned the corridor. When she was sure the coast was clear, she hurried back to the kitchen where she poured another mug of coffee so she had a reason to be downstairs.

Carrying the mug, she went out to the sunporch where several of the women were gathered. Pam was absent, but Dolly was among them and Gillian complimented her on the new hairstyle. That led to a discussion of hair and makeup and the pros and cons of cosmetic surgery. Gillian was glad to join in. She didn't want to think about Alexander McMullin. She'd almost made another bad mistake. She was letting herself feel dependent on him. He might be out there in the van watching out for her. And that was making him feel protective. But she knew from experience that everything would change once the drug dealers were put out of business.

And another thing she knew from experience. Alexander McMullin had the power to break her heart, if she let herself care about him too much.

So she had to keep her distance. Emotionally. But how could she do that when he was her lifeline to the outside world? When every time she spoke a sentence in her room, she imagined him listening in?

Too bad the only way to get a message out to Lieutenant LeBarron was over the transmitter. She'd like to tell him she wanted somebody else on surveillance detail. But she wasn't going to use tricks to get Alex back in here. She was going to finish up her undercover job and get back to her patrol cop duties—where she belonged.

Chapter Nine

Alex strode back to the van, hoping his poker face was in place.

"You were gone for a long time. I was starting to worry," Seth said.

"No problems," he reassured him. "I got a chance to nose around one of the offices."

"Find anything good?"

"I've photographed the pages of a book Gillian found in the desk drawer."

"Gillian—you hooked up with her."

"Yeah," he said, then went back to the book. "The notations are in code. I'd like to get them back to headquarters where somebody else can analyze the data."

"Let me drop you off there," Seth offered.

"Appreciate it," Alex answered.

As soon as he entered the building, he went straight to Conrad Burke's office.

"You look like a man with a mission," the director commented, glancing up from his desk.

"I've got some film that could be significant." Succinctly, he reported on the book that he and Gillian had discovered.

"Drop it off at the lab on the way out."

"I already did. And we need to check out a greasy-looking guy named Gaspard. Gillian says he's the real owner of the bordello, or he works for the real owner."

"What's his first name?"

"She doesn't know."

Conrad made a note about Gaspard, then leaned back in his chair. "I've got some information for you, too."

"From the look on your face, I wouldn't say it was good."

"The amount of Category Five in New Orleans has increased dramatically since that contingent from Nilia arrived in town. Could be a coincidence but we're not ruling out the possibility that that's where the stuff is coming from."

"Can we do anything about it?" Alex asked. "Like arrest their asses? Some grueling interrogation sessions might do wonders for the Category Five investigation."

"I'd love to. But they're being careful. As far as we can tell, they haven't done anything illegal."

They kicked around various ideas for several minutes.

That got Alex thinking that if he were a dirty cop, he'd go out and plant some evidence that would get the rebels hauled down to the station house. Getting arrested might make them think twice about making the Crescent City the focus of their operation—regardless of what that operation was.

"What?" Conrad asked, and Alex realized that he'd been sitting across from his boss, hatching plots that were better left to a spy movie.

"I was just thinking that we need to figure out a way to get them," he murmured.

The head of operations nodded. "We could probably

bring them in on something minor, but then we'd miss the big cheese.''

''Yeah,'' Alex agreed. He knew Conrad was angry because he wanted to get the bastards responsible for what had happened to Wiley Longbottom. Alex had only met Longbottom on the night they'd all gone to Bourbon Street Libations. So he didn't have the same feelings for the man that Conrad possessed. His own concerns were different.

As he finally extracted himself from the office, he was thinking about Gillian. The more drugs in town, the more danger for her. Like, were they going to ask her to give the stuff to a customer? He hoped she'd have to work there for a few weeks before they trusted her to do that. And in a few weeks, she'd better be out of there. Or—

That alternative made his mouth go dry. He'd known all along that Gillian was stepping into quicksand. More than ever, he wanted to yank her the hell to solid ground. But that wasn't his call. They were in the middle of a covert operation and they were both going to have to see it through.

RICARDO GONZALEZ PAUSED to admire the sweetly gurgling fountain at the end of the sunroom. In the center of a round marble basin, a cherub was peeing into the water. He loved the whimsy of the figure.

In fact, the whole indoor garden was charming. It was in the back of a sixteen-room house in the area of town he'd learned was called the Garden District. He'd bought the mansion, furnishings included, for his New Orleans headquarters. And he planned to leave a contingent of men here when he left again for Nilia.

He wasn't sure when that would be. It mostly depended on how fast his various deals were firmed up. He might have to kill his current U.S. partner. But that wouldn't be a problem. He could easily get rid of the man if he proved to be uncooperative and find someone else who was more cooperative.

Until things settled down, he'd have to stay here. But really, it was a very nice environment. When he got home, he'd have to build himself several rooms like this—in his most important mansions.

And there were some other touches he'd take back with him. Like the painted ceilings and the Greek columns in the living room. Perhaps he could persuade an architect from this city to move down to Nilia.

Perhaps he should start Pedro looking for someone suitable. Someone who had a secret to hide. Someone who would go along with the deal because he had no choice.

Ricardo walked around the fountain to the back door and stood gazing out at one of the gardeners who was trimming some of the hedges. The whole garden was a marvel. So lush and rich. And surrounded by a brick wall that gave perfect privacy.

Satisfied with his domain, he strolled back to the little office off the dining room and picked up the report he'd received this morning.

According to his plant manager, things were going well back home. The man was a business genius. He'd found a cheaper supply of the raw ingredient for the product that was already getting a reputation in New Orleans.

And the chemist who cooked the compounds into that special Nilian brew was performing admirably. Of course, it helped to have the man's wife and children in prison. He'd promised to release them when they could find a replacement for the chemist. But he wasn't in any hurry. Slave labor was always a fine arrangement.

WELL, ANOTHER FUN-FILLED day in the McDonough Club, Gillian thought as she finished a cup of afternoon tea on the sunporch. Half closing her eyes, she tried to pretend that she was a guest in an elegant mansion. And that Alex was in the chair beside her. As it often did, her mind drifted to him—pretending they were having a conversation.

She didn't want to talk about her life as she was living it now. And dwelling on their few months together made her feel too vulnerable. So she silently told him stories from her past. Like the time she'd stolen a piece of cake from the kitchen and hidden it in her room—and the ants had gotten to it. Mom had caught her throwing it in the trash. She'd told Gillian that was a lesson in honesty.

She switched to better memories and told him about the time she'd gotten to be the fairy princess in the school play and Mom had made her a crown covered with aluminum foil. And they'd pasted on sequins they'd gotten from the dollar store.

She grinned to herself and told him another story about Dad helping her learn to ride a bike. Or the times Dad had brought home produce from the grocery store that was on the edge of going bad, but Mom had been able to cook it up and use it just fine.

Thinking about the good times helped ground her. Helped her cope with the nights and days in this place that were falling into a distinct pattern. In the evenings she took men up to her room and drugged them. While they were sleeping, she searched their clothing and reported their names and anything of interest to the agents listening in the van. When the johns woke up, she told them they'd been fantastic in bed. She still hated the work. But she wasn't as nervous about it as she had been in the beginning. In fact, she was downright pleased with how well she was pulling it off.

By day she interacted with the other women in the house

and tried to collect more information on the drug distribution operation. Mostly she got along with everybody, although a few times Babs had gone out of her way to make some cutting remarks. Gillian had ignored them, although she'd wondered what she'd done to set the woman off.

She kept the question to herself, because it wasn't important enough to mention it to Alex. Or whoever was out there in the van, watching over her.

After looking over her shoulders she stepped into a back corridor. There were quite a few rooms she hadn't explored. And she was making a point of searching a new one each day. Maybe she'd get lucky and find a stash of the drug hidden in one of the antique chests, she speculated with a snort. They were more likely locked in the madam's office. But she couldn't exactly search there.

She had learned to be aware of her surroundings at all times. She had taken only a few steps down the hallway, when she picked up on voices coming from behind one of the closed doors. Stopping short, she cupped her hand around her ear and leaned toward the door. One of the speakers was a strident-sounding man who was obviously ordering someone around. Was Gaspard back? She hadn't seen him for a few days. And she'd almost wiped away that feeling of revulsion he'd given her. She had hoped never to see him again.

Now she froze in place, wondering what to do. Back away? Or try to figure out what was going on in the room.

Hearing the rasp of the doorknob, she ducked quickly around the corner and pressed her shoulders against the wall.

She'd thought of a cover story earlier. She had a headache, and one of the other women had told her there was aspirin in the medicine cabinet in the bathroom down here.

As she heard someone step into the hall, the story sounded flimsy.

Her heart blocking her windpipe, Gillian waited for footsteps to come in her direction. But they went the other way and she felt as though she'd made a miraculous escape.

Risking a peek around the corner, she saw Frank standing in the hallway. He wasn't as threatening as Gaspard, but still she didn't want him to know she was there—spying.

Luckily, his attention was focused firmly on a woman—Dolly, to be exact. He had her arm in a grip that looked like it might leave a bruise.

"I don't like going to that bar," Dolly was saying.

"Too bad."

"Why can't one of the other girls do it this time?" she whined.

"'Cause it's your turn, and you're good at reeling them in." He gave a nasty laugh. "I guess you have a way with druggies."

"But…"

"The way I heard it, a lot more of you girls will be going out to the bars," Frank snapped. "Not just from this house."

A door closed and the sound of the voices was muffled now.

What bar? Was Dolly being sent to Bourbon Street Libations? Did she have the job of bringing men here who had been dosed by Jack the bartender? And did Frank's remark mean that they were expanding the operation?

There was no way of knowing that.

She tried to think about the girls she'd met here. There were about fifteen of them. And they were never all in the lounge at the same time, even at the beginning of the evening. Did that mean that most of them were being rotated to bar duty—except for the new hire who was still on probation? Were they bringing in men who had been drugged like Wiley Longbottom?

Gillian edged toward the corner of the hallway, wondering if she could hear any more. She had taken only a couple of steps when someone called her name.

"Gillian?"

Struggling not to look guilty, she swung back toward the parlor. Pam was standing at the end of the hall. Pam again. Funny how she was always turning up. But at least it wasn't Babs. Probably she would have called the madam to ask Gillian why she was out of the part of the house that the women frequented.

Now she pasted an inquisitive look on her face. "Yes?"

"There's a guy asking for you."

She took a quick look at her watch. They weren't on duty for another two hours. "But it's still early."

"I know. Apparently he heard you were great, and he's leaving town this evening. So he came in and made a special request."

"How does he even know about me? I've only been here a week?"

"I guess you're already getting a reputation for being an excellent bed partner, you know."

"Oh great," Gillian muttered under her breath. It was so early that she hadn't yet taken the antidote to the drug that she gave her customers. Now what was she going to do?

"Look like you're happy as a lark," Pam advised.

"Right."

Keeping her expression open, she walked rapidly back down the hall, glad that she was dressed and not wearing a robe.

In the doorway to the parlor, she glanced around. It was too early for the usual crowd of women and their customers. There were just Madam Dupré, looking a little anxious, and one man standing by the window with his back to the room.

"Gillian, I'm glad you could join us," the madam said.

"I'm sorry. I wasn't quite ready," Gillian said, aware that Pam hadn't gone back to her room.

"I understand. I appreciate your coming down a little early."

The man who had been talking to the mistress of the house was now looking eagerly toward the door. As his gaze fixed on Gillian, she felt goose bumps rise on her bare arms. She'd been thinking it was good she was dressed. Now she felt like she might not have bothered, because this guy was obviously peeling away her clothing with his sharp gaze. Most guys were more subtle in the parlor. But he zeroed in on her breasts and she had to press her arms to her sides to keep from folding them across her chest.

The john looking at her as if she were a piece of prime steak in the meat cooler was short and heavy, somewhere in his fifties, she judged, with thinning dark hair pasted across the top of his head. A gold pin shone in the lapel of what was obviously an expensive suit. And she caught the strong smell of garlic on his breath.

"Charles is one of our most valued customers. He was anxious to get together with you," Madam Dupré said.

Gillian managed to make a small uming sound. She disliked this man on sight. But no one had ever told her if it was all right to refuse an offer of employment within the boundaries she'd set, and she suspected that she would be in big trouble if she tried it now. Especially with a customer that the madam valued.

"I'm so honored that you asked for me," she said sweetly.

"My friend Jimmy told me you're the best."

Jimmy. Well, she knew he'd left her room thinking they'd had a great time in bed.

"How flattering."

"Why don't you two go upstairs," the madam suggested. "Charles has a plane to catch later this evening."

"Of course," Gillian agreed.

He crossed the room, and as she turned, he flattened his fleshy palm against her bare back. It was all she could do to keep from cringing.

Her teeth were clenched as she climbed the stairs, her mind scrambling for some way to get out of this situation. Up till now, she'd felt like she was handling this job. Until today she'd avoided having sex with any of the men who had come to her room. But always before she'd taken the antidote. This afternoon she hadn't had a chance yet. Now what was she going to do?

"Which way?" the man behind her asked, and she realized that she'd stopped at the top of the steps.

BABS STARTED TO STEP OUT of her room, then stepped back and pulled the door closed, so that there was only a narrow crack. In the hallway she could see Gillian Stanwick with Charles.

Charles!

She'd been thinking she was going to see him soon. She'd been thinking that maybe he liked her enough to get her out of this place. Set her up somewhere in town in a nice apartment. He'd talked about doing that. Now here he was sauntering down the hall after Gillian Stanwick like she was the Pied Piper and he was a rat!

Usually when he came here, he asked for her. But obviously his good friend had told him about that new bitch. And he wanted to try her out.

What was so special about her, anyway? She was pretty.

But she wasn't a real looker. Did she do something kinky in bed? What? One thing Babs knew: she was going to make Gillian Stanwick wish she'd never set foot in this house.

"THIS WAY." Gillian led the john down the hall, then ushered him into the room.

As soon as she'd closed the door, he reached for her, lowering his mouth.

"You know we're not allowed to kiss," she said sharply, pushing at his chest.

"I thought if I gave you a nice big tip, you'd be willing to give me some extra consideration."

"I'm afraid I can't break Madam Dupré's rules. I haven't been here long, and I want to keep my job."

"I wouldn't want to get you in trouble," he said, his voice knife-edged.

"Thank you."

"Take off your dress," he said with a commanding note in his voice. "I want to see what you've got."

She had hoped she could offer him a drink when they got up here so she could palm a tablet and take the antidote. Now she knew she'd be taking too big a risk by going against his wishes. Madam Dupré had made it clear this man had better give a good account of their time together.

Fighting not to clench her jaw, she reached for the zipper at the back of her dress. As she pulled at the tab, she imagined Alex listening to the gruff order her guest had issued.

Don't come rushing in here, Alex, she silently pleaded. *I can handle this, and if you burst in, you could blow my cover.*

ALEX SWORE, turning the air blue in the surveillance van. He'd been spending every evening listening to Gillian in her bedroom with a succession of slimeball guys who wanted to get their jollies with a prostitute. The strain was tearing him apart. And Rich had suggested that he take a break. But he'd stuck with the assignment, because not knowing what was going on was worse than having to listen to the action.

Now he conjured up an image of the scene behind Gillian's closed door and he felt his throat constrict. "A kiss!" he rasped. "What the hell is going on in there? First she's off the mike for forty minutes. Next thing, she's upstairs with a john—in the damn afternoon."

He reached to turn up the volume. "It's much too early for her to be working. Listen to her. I'll bet she hasn't even taken the antidote."

Behind him, Rich murmured something that could have been agreement.

"I'm going in there."

As soon as the declaration was out of Alex's mouth, his partner put a restraining hand on his shoulder. "Give it a few minutes. If she gets into trouble with that guy, you can scare the spit out of him with the fire bell."

Alex glanced back at the other New Orleans Confidential agent, thinking that the tactic might work. Since Gillian had moved into the house, they'd rigged a remote control that would turn on the fire alarm. "Okay. But I'm not going to let that bastard paw her up."

Gillian's voice blared out from the microphone, making Alex jump, and he reached to quickly turn the volume down again so that passersby on the street wouldn't hear the conversation in the private bedroom.

The john was speaking again. "Now take off your bra. I want to see those nice tits of yours."

Her answer came out cool and collected. "Just let me get a drink of water first."

He heard water running and hoped to hell she was taking the antidote to the drug. But even after she did, she was going to have to wait fifteen minutes before she could give the guy the amnesiac stuff.

"That's better," the man's voice finally said, and Alex winced as he pictured Gillian standing there with her breasts bare.

What did this particular slimeball look like? He imagined a guy with powerful muscles who could overpower Gillian if she refused to cooperate.

His attention snapped back to the microphone as Gillian spoke again, her voice low and intimate. "Let me tell you an idea I have for something special," she purred. "Something I think you're going to like."

"Yeah? What?"

"A little game a lot of my clients have found very exciting. Have you ever had a woman tie you up? And then do very erotic things to your body."

"I've never done anything like that."

"I guarantee that surrendering completely to a woman's touch is very stimulating."

"You guarantee that?" he asked, his tone insinuating.

"Absolutely," she answered warmly.

"Well, if I don't like being tied up, we can try it the other way. I'll handcuff you to the headboard."

"That's fine."

Alex swore again. "I thought she told the madam she wouldn't do that."

"She's not going to do it now. She's got him on the hook. Give her a chance to reel him in," Rich whispered.

Alex clamped his fingers around the edge of the table, welcoming the feel of the hard metal digging into his hand.

Over the microphone came a noise that sounded like a case being opened.

The man's nervous voice followed almost immediately. "What are those?"

"Just ropes. Part of my bondage kit. Why don't you take off your clothes, lie down and get comfortable."

"And we can stop any time I want?" he asked, an edge of nerves in his voice.

"Of course. You're the one in complete control."

Rich snorted. "Yeah. Way to go, girl." He glanced at Alex and grinned. The grin grew wider as they both heard the rustle of clothing, then the creak of bedsprings.

"That looks so erotic," Gillian cooed. "Just let me secure your wrists and ankles. I'll use easy knots, so we can untie you quickly if that's what you want. But I don't think you'll ask to be untied until I've had my wicked way with you."

Alex waited with his stomach in knots as they listened to her moving around. She was humming as she worked. Then she was whispering low sexy words that made Alex lower his eyes toward the table. What the hell was she doing to the guy? He burned to know, yet at the same time, he didn't like the picture etching itself into his brain.

"Are you comfortable?" Gillian purred.

"Yes."

There was a pause and Alex strained to hear what was going on. "I love your chest."

"Um."

"That feels good, doesn't it?"

"You know it does, baby," the man answered, his voice slightly slurred.

"Thank God," Alex breathed. "She gave him the stuff."

"I told you she knows what she's doing," Rich crowed.

"Yeah," Alex answered, acting like he hadn't been about to jump out of his skin as he listened to what was going on in the room.

GILLIAN LOOKED DOWN with distaste at the whalelike body sprawled on her bed. This guy had given her the willies when he was fully dressed. Naked, he was positively repulsive. But she'd rendered him harmless. She hoped.

Spinning on her heel, she picked up the bra that she'd recently discarded. After putting it on, she took down the lacy robe hanging on the back of the inside of the bedroom door. Then she turned back to the man who was trussed like a sacrificial buffalo.

"You're sleeping very nicely," she said, watching Charles's face. But really, she was speaking for Alex. The whole time she'd been in here with her guest, she'd been half expecting Alex to come bursting into the room shouting, "Police! Freeze."

Now she wanted him to know that everything was under control.

"You'll sleep for about half an hour," she said to Charles. "And when you start to wake up, I'll tell you how much fun we had together. You'll leave here perfectly satisfied with my performance. And you'll give me high marks when you tell Madam Dupré what a good time you had with me."

She hoped she'd calmed Alex down. Easing onto the bed, she whispered some more suggestions. Then she did her usual check of the john's pockets and relayed the personal information to Alex.

"He's Charles Pringle," she said. "He has a small chain of grocery stores in Indiana. And a couple of hits of cocaine in his shirt pocket. Maybe you can make sure he's searched at the airport and arrested," she added with satisfaction.

When she'd finished with her task, she moved to the chair in the corner, picked up a magazine from the table next to it and tried to focus on the details of a French country house. It was an exercise in futility. She was too wired to focus on the magazine—or anything else.

Finally, after half an hour, she shrugged out of the clothing she'd put on and went back to the bed. Gritting her teeth, she stroked the guy's shoulder.

"You're going to wake up soon," she murmured. "You were so sexy. I had a wonderful time with you. And I know you had a good time, too."

Then she told him some of the things she had supposedly done to him. As she talked, she undid his bonds and arranged his arms at his sides. When he opened his eyes and blinked at her, she gave him a brilliant smile.

"That was fantastic, don't you think?"

"Yes," he said thickly.

"We had a great time, and you don't have to worry about missing your plane."

He sat up and reached for the clothing that she'd laid neatly on the end of the bed.

ALEX SAT WITH his teeth gritted as he listened to the dialogue in the bedroom. Gillian had pulled off another coup. He had to give her that. But she'd been in deep trouble before she'd given that guy the sleeping potion.

"Come see me the next time you're in town," Gillian said, and he heard the satisfaction in her voice.

"Oh, I will." The john sounded equally satisfied. Too bad Alex McMullin was sitting in a van parked around the corner feeling like razor wire was twisting in his gut. He would like nothing better than to have airport security catch the guy with the coke in his pocket. But he wanted him out of town—away from New Orleans. Away from Gillian.

He glanced at his watch, expecting that she would start getting ready for the rest of the evening. Instead, he heard her clear her throat.

When she spoke, her voice was low. "Something happened a while ago. I was downstairs, and Frank was talking to Dolly. He told her she was going back to the bar to reel them in. I think he meant Bourbon Street Libations. She didn't want to go, but he told her she didn't have a choice. So maybe you can send someone over there to look for her. She's a small blonde with shoulder-length hair. Done in a flip."

Gillian sighed. "I can't even be sure anyone can hear me," she said, sounding depressed.

"I hear you," he murmured, wishing they had two-way communications. But that would be too dangerous for her, of course.

MADAM DUPRÉ was sitting at the desk in her comfortable office when the phone rang. Perhaps it was another special customer. A customer who would pay extra for the services of one of her girls. But when she saw the name on the Caller ID, her expression of happy anticipation vanished. It was Gaspard—again.

He'd already called a little while ago to personally give some order. What did he want *now?* Lately he'd been stopping by and calling with orders every other day, and she didn't like that. If the man would simply let her run the business the way she knew how, everything would go more smoothly. But he was on edge—nervous about something. And he wouldn't tell her what.

She considered having Wilma take the call. But she knew her boss would be insulted by talking to the maid. So she sighed and pasted a smile into her voice.

"Maurice, it's good to hear from you again."

He made a noise that could have been agreement.

"What can I do for you?" she asked, forcing herself not to add the word "now."

"I just learned that we will be hosting a special party," he said. "Eight guys who are looking for a fun time."

"Good."

"This one's being arranged by J.S. Of course, we're going to give him a big discount."

"A discount! That's ridiculous. This place is expensive to run. I have to pay the girls, pay the liquor bill, the food bill—"

He cut her off. "Are you questioning my judgment?"

"No. Of course not," she answered, licking her dry lips.

"Good, because I could get someone else in there to run the club."

"No," she said quickly, hearing the note of panic in her own voice. She needed this job until she was able to squirrel away enough for a comfortable retirement.

"Then follow my orders," he said in the deadly quiet tone that she had grown to hate. When she'd agreed to run this house, she hadn't known that Maurice Gaspard was part of the deal.

"Of course," she agreed, wishing that she could put out a contract on the man. Did she dare?

Gaspard was speaking again, giving orders about getting the house ready for the guests as if she didn't know how to do that. But she took notes, wondering if she could cut corners on the food and liquor.

"And what about that new girl, Gillian Seymour?" he asked, his voice still low.

"What about her?"

"How is she performing?"

"Very well. She's quite popular with the men. She has a special guest this afternoon, a man who asked for her specifically—on the recommendation of one of his friends."

"All right. But I want to look at the tapes from her room."

"Yes, of course," she answered, thinking that she'd better get the camera in room eight working. It had been out of commission off and on since the girl arrived. She'd have to get Frank to go up there again. But not now, of course.

However, waiting created a problem. Gaspard had said he wanted to see some footage, and she'd better have some to show him.

Chapter Ten

The blond girl lay on her narrow bed, pretending to be so worn out that there was nothing she could do besides sleep. She'd been using that tactic for the past few days, and she was thinking that it could only work for so long.

She'd made a big mistake by letting that greasy-haired guy chat her up on the street. But he'd told her he worked for an organization that helped kids in trouble. Still, she hadn't quite trusted him—not for him to take her anywhere. Although she'd let him buy her some food from an outdoor hotdog stand. Which should have been safe.

But the bastard had managed to slip something into her drink—something that had made her woozy. She'd tried to run, then had ended up slumping against him. When she'd woken up, she'd found herself in this hellhole, and she knew she had to get out before something really bad happened.

Someone came to the door, but she kept her eyes closed, praying that they'd go away. And the footsteps receded. Heavy footsteps. One of the men who was in charge of this basement prison.

She'd asked one of the other girls, a little bit of a thing named Sally, how to get out of here.

Sally had shrugged. "There ain't no way. Until they're through with you and toss you out."

"I'm getting away."

"Good luck. If they catch you, they'll wupp your hide."

She'd given the other girl a defiant look, but her insides had been twisting themselves in knots. At least she'd found something in the medicine cabinet that she'd been able to use. A laxative. It would give her the runs. And she was going to take it, as soon as she got over the sleeping sickness bit. The runs were a good excuse to keep her out of some guy's bed. Some guy who liked teenage girls. Like her stepfather. That's why she was here. She'd tried to get away from a bad situation and she'd ended up in worse trouble.

Meanwhile, she was praying that she'd figure a way out before anything really gross happened.

CONRAD BURKE LOOKED DOWN at the folder on his desk. In it were the latest medical reports on Wiley Longbottom. The hospital was keeping NOC in the loop. But, really, there was no change in the former Colorado Department of Public Safety director's condition. And the longer he stayed unconscious, the worse the prognosis.

Conrad closed his eyes for a moment. In a frantic effort to find the bastards who had put Wiley in the hospital, he'd rushed New Orleans Confidential into operation months before they'd planned to be up and running. Since then, he'd had occasion to wonder if he'd made a mistake. If they'd waited and gotten themselves better prepared, would they be further ahead now?

Standing up, he walked to the window and looked out at weeds baking in the sun. The view matched his present mood. He wasn't sure how long he'd been standing there when the phone rang and he turned back to the desk. When he saw from the Caller ID that Police Chief Henri Courville was on the line, he stifled a groan.

"Just what I need," he muttered, then cleared his throat, adopting a commanding tone as he picked up the receiver. "Burke here."

"Henri Courville."

"What can I do for you, Chief?"

"How long are you going to keep one of my cops playing prostitute in that bordello?"

Conrad held his temper. The chief had loved the idea of the undercover operation when it had first been proposed. Now he was acting like he wanted immediate results. "We're getting a better handle on the prostitute operation."

"What specifically?"

"We have a code book that your officer and one of our agents were able to photograph."

"And?"

"We think it may be a list of clients."

"But you don't know for sure," Courville snapped.

"We're working on it." He debated mentioning the underage prostitutes Gillian Seymour had reported were in the house, then decided it was better to keep that piece of information to himself.

"Seymour has been working undercover at the bordello for two weeks. I may want to pull her out of there. It's only a matter of time before that girl gets herself in trouble."

That girl? Was that how the chief thought of his police officer? Of course, the chief had a point. In fact, Gillian Seymour had had a close call a few days earlier. But she'd gotten herself out of hot water with some pretty clever maneuvering.

Instead of sharing that news, he said, "If you shut her

down, you'll cancel weeks of work. She's just now coming up with some information we can use.''

"Like what?"

"She's confirmed that the prostitutes going after the drugged Category Five customers are from the McDonough Club," Conrad said, glad that he'd read Alex's reports as soon as they'd arrived on his desk.

"She has to do better than that."

"Undercover operations take time," Conrad reminded him.

"Are you telling me how to do my job?" Courville snapped.

"Of course not," Conrad answered in what he hoped was a conciliatory tone.

"Don't worry—we're working this case from all angles to find out where the drugs are coming from and what's running the show."

"I'm listening," Courville said.

"To that end, we're keeping a close eye on the Nilia rebels. It might be a long shot but these two investigations could be linked somehow. Our sources tell us that more of the drugs have been on the streets since the rebels paid us a visit."

"I need more to go on than speculation!" Courville demanded.

Changing tactics, Conrad couldn't keep himself from asking, "I was wondering if you'd made any progress in identifying the dead guy stuffed into the trunk of that car?"

"Not yet," Courville growled. "It's a difficult case since his fingerprints were missing. I'll let you know as soon as we get an ID."

"I appreciate that," Conrad answered, again keeping his voice mild, although he was sure that the police chief had taken his point.

"I haven't seen any of the reports from your surveillance team at the bordello," the chief said pointedly, putting the heat back on Conrad.

"I assumed you wouldn't want to plow through the day-to-day operations."

"I'd appreciate seeing a copy of what you have to date."

"Of course. I'll get them to you as soon as possible," Conrad said, thinking that he was going to be up all night editing the text to take out sensitive information.

TWO DAYS AFTER the incident with Charles Pringle, Gillian was heading back to her room when she heard footsteps on the stairs behind her. Looking around, she saw it was Pam, who had a strained expression on her face.

"What's wrong?" she asked, trying not to sound like her throat had suddenly clogged.

"Nothing," Pam insisted.

"You don't look like it's nothing."

"Madam Dupré said to tell everyone to take special care with their appearance tonight. We're having honored guests," she added somewhat breathlessly. .

"Who?"

Pam looked over her shoulder. "Some important guys."

"If we're supposed to look our best, maybe you can give me some advice on what to wear," Gillian said.

Pam hesitated for a moment. "Okay."

Gillian led the way to her room, then ushered the other woman inside. She hadn't been out of the McDonough Club since she'd arrived, and she only had the outfits she'd brought with her. But that wasn't her *only* reason for asking Pam to her room. She wanted to know what was going on.

Opening her closet, she began sorting through the collection of working-girl outfits. "So, are these rich guys? What should I try for? Elegant?"

Pam laughed. "Skimpy. Sexy. Provocative is more like it." She walked to the closet and pulled out a dress with shiny blue spangles that would dip low over the breasts. The skirt was long but slit up to the hips so that lots of leg would show with every step she took. "Wear this blue one. The color will be good on you."

"Where it covers my skin, you mean," Gillian answered, a sardonic note in her voice.

Pam laughed again. "Yeah. But, you know, it's part of the deal working here."

Gillian nodded. "So what can you tell me about this special company?"

"All I know is that they're important visitors. We get them from time to time. And we're paraded out as a special treat."

"For whom?"

"Sometimes I think they're people who are part of the city establishment."

"You mean, public officials."

"Sometimes."

"Like who?" Gillian persisted, hoping she wasn't going too far with her questions.

Pam glanced toward the door as though someone might be in the hall, listening. Lowering her voice, she said, "It's better not to be too nosy. But I did hear Madam Dupré asking which of us spoke Spanish. So I assume that would be a plus with these guys."

That got Gillian's attention. Spanish. Like the thugs from Nilia?

Pam looked toward the closed door again. "The last time we had special company…one of the girls got hurt."

"Badly?"

"They took her to the hospital. The guy she was entertaining did something to her. We never did know what."

Gillian's heart had started pounding.

"If one of them picks you, be careful."

"Okay. Thanks for the tip. How many of them are coming?"

"I don't know." Pam glanced toward the door. "I'd better get ready."

Gillian hesitated, then introduced a topic that had been nagging at her for several days.

"I want to ask you about Babs," she said.

"What about her?"

"Everyone here has been pretty nice to me. But she's always acting hostile. Do you have any idea why?"

Pam gave a tight nod. "You threaten her."

"How? I haven't done anything."

"I know. You wouldn't. But she's getting a little old for this business. The guys aren't asking for her as often as they used to. On the other hand, you're getting a lot of attention."

"Oh," Gillian murmured. "What should I do?"

"There's nothing you can do—except stay out of her way."

"Thanks for the advice," she said, thinking that it wasn't going to do her a lot of good. This house might be relatively large, but there was no way to completely avoid anyone—especially when the women who worked here all congregated in the lounge in the evenings.

"And thanks for listening," Gillian said.

"Any time."

Pam departed, leaving Gillian standing by the closet staring at the blue dress. She might have cursed under her breath, but she was afraid Alex would pick it up, and she didn't want him to worry about her.

"Nice turn of events," she said instead, picturing him sitting at the metal table in the van.

Of course, maybe he was on another assignment. There was no way of knowing, because she hadn't seen him since the day he'd come in to deliver coffee and then had pretended he was her boyfriend. He'd taken her in his arms that day. Now it seemed like he was deliberately staying away from her.

She canceled that thought. It wasn't fair to second guess him. He couldn't keep barging in here just because she wanted to see him.

Just because she was dependent on him. As soon as that idea leaped into her head, she tried to banish it, too. Lord, had she ever been so off balance?

She was isolated in this house, and he was her contact point with the world—with law and order. Sometimes, after she was finished with her duties, she lay in bed and pretended that he was there—next to her. All she'd have to do was stretch out her hand and she could touch him. Like when she'd been a kid. She'd shared a bed with her sister, Ginny. Sometimes she'd resented not having a bed to herself. And sometimes she'd been glad to have a friend and confidante next to her. With Alex, it was all a fantasy. And if he wasn't in her bedroom, maybe he wasn't really out there listening.

Grimly, she pulled out the piece of equipment that looked like a compact and held it up, pretending to check her appearance in the small mirror. In actuality, she was checking on the hidden camera that she'd disabled when she'd arrived. Several times a day she checked to make sure it still failed to function.

She knew that Frank had been in here more than once, on the pretext of changing light bulbs and doing other routine maintenance. Once or twice he'd fixed the camera, but she'd always disabled it again after a few hours. Since it was off now, she risked a direct comment about the night's visitors.

"So what do you think?" she murmured as she took the dress off the rack and laid it on the bed. "Who are these mysterious guys who speak Spanish? Too bad you can't go upstairs in the building across the street and hold up a sign in the window, so we can pass messages."

That image triggered a laugh that sounded on the edge of hysteria. Immediately, she clapped her hand over her mouth. She didn't want him to think she was scared or off balance or anything. She wanted him to think she was fine—even if it was a lie. And she wanted to know how the investigation was going.

With a grimace, she marched into the bathroom and took her special vitamin, the antidote to the drug that she'd be giving to her customer.

IN THE VAN, Alex sat with his full attention on the speaker.

He didn't like that laugh Gillian had tried to bite back. Not at all. The situation was getting to her. Which was normal, he told himself. Especially with the announcement that a bunch of Spanish-speaking johns were about to arrive.

Especially when he could very easily imagine the working conditions. He'd seen Gillian's wardrobe, and he knew what blue dress she and Pam had been talking about. An indecent little number that somebody should have thrown in the trash.

"McMullin?"

He turned his head, realizing that Rich had been speaking to him.

"Yeah?"

"Do you think those special guests are our friends from Nilia?" the former navy SEAL asked.

Alex ran a frustrated hand through his hair. "Yeah. It's too bad we can't make her cue card idea work."

"Mmm, hmm," Rich agreed.

"This whole gig would have been easier if she could have left the house—like to go shopping or something."

"Yeah," Alex growled. That was an unexpected problem. Because when he'd first seen the prostitutes in Bourbon Street Libations, he'd assumed that they could go out. Apparently that was only true for certain women—those who were trusted in the Category Five distribution part of the operation.

Gillian hadn't been included in that. And much as he hated to admit it, the arrival of these special visitors might be their big chance to get some information. She had more than one drug with her. In combination with her amnesiac cream, she had something that would encourage a guy to talk. But it was more dangerous to use the combination, and he didn't know whether she should do it or not. There was no way to discuss it with her. But if she did get one of those guys to sing, maybe they could call a halt to this whole miserable charade.

WILMA, THE MAID, was in the hall ringing a small, tinkly bell. It might be a subtle signal, but Gillian knew that she must obey the summons.

"Time to meet the special company," she said, hoping she didn't sound too breathless.

Pulling open the door, she stepped into the hall. Other women were already there, heading for the stairs, and she hurried to join them, almost colliding with Babs, who shouldered her out of the way. She gave the redhead a startled look but stepped back, anxious not to make waves. Because she'd moved out of the way, she now had to hurry to catch up, feeling like a high school freshman late to class.

But they weren't going to any class. Not dressed in a assortment of outfits that would make a stripper proud. Apparently everybody had gotten the word to dress in their skimpiest outfits tonight.

The women at the front reached the bottom of the stairs and slowed their pace as they headed into the parlor. Gillian was one of the last to enter.

In a heartbeat, she took in the scene. Madam Dupré was at one side of the room. But she was in the background. Standing by the door, inspecting each woman who came in, was Gaspard.

Gillian wanted to cast her eyes down. But she kept her gaze steady as she focused on the other occupants of the parlor.

Lounging around the room was an assortment of short, dark, muscular men, avidly inspecting each woman as she stepped into the room. The men were all dressed in dark, short-sleeved shirts and dark slacks, as though the outfits were some kind of uniform. And, in fact, they looked like they could be part of somebody's private army.

That might simply be her own fanciful interpretation. But she wanted to pass the observation by Alex.

As she glanced at the men, one thing was obvious: they were primed for the evening's entertainment.

"Our guests want a good look at you. Line up," Gaspard said in a low voice that was chilling precisely because it assumed obedience.

The other women instantly followed directions, and Gillian joined them as they arranged themselves along the far wall like mannequins in a showroom.

She could see the eager gleam in the eyes of the men. They were all looking over the feminine merchandise as though the women were being exhibited for their personal enjoyment—which was basically true.

Several took a step forward as they made their inspection. One walked up to Dolly and boldly stroked his hand over her breast, making the man on his right laugh appreciatively and follow suit with Lisa.

Another of the men stood with his arms folded across his chest, his gaze traveling rapidly over the line of working girls. He'd barely given the rest of the group a quick look when his attention snapped back to Gillian, and she felt the breath solidify in her lungs, so that it was suddenly difficult to breathe.

She'd thought Charles from two days ago was creepy. He might have been a fuzzy cartoon character compared to the man who was sliding his gaze over her now as though he'd already bought and paid for her body.

She didn't know whether it was better to meet his eyes or glance away. He looked like he'd come up from the street. Now he had acquired a thin layer of civilization that barely concealed the dark currents below the surface.

When he came striding toward her, she lifted her chin.

"I like your looks, *señorita*," he said, his Spanish accent very obvious. "And I like a woman who is bold enough to acknowledge her man's attention."

"I like your looks, too," she lied. "And your take-charge attitude. Can I get you a drink?"

"I think not. I want to go up to your room where we can get naked together."

Well, that was certainly direct, she thought, noting Gaspard's smirk. He was apparently listening in and getting some enjoyment from the situation.

Other couples had paired off, and some of the men had escorted their partners to the bar. The noise level in the room was increasing dramatically as men and women got to know each other. Her date wanted to get right to business.

"Of course," she answered.

As she and the guy left the room, she saw that Babs was standing alone with no partner—and looking daggers in her direction.

Swiftly, she turned away, leading her customer toward the stairs that she'd descended so recently, feeling his breath on her neck, and immediately she forgot all about Babs.

She was starting to hate this walk to her room with an eager man breathing down her back. More than that, she hated the moment when the door clanked closed behind them like a jailhouse gate. She and the man would be in here for an hour, and it was up to her to make sure nothing happened that she couldn't handle. What if this guy wanted to stay longer?

After closing the door, she turned to face her new companion and said, "My name is Gillian. What's yours?"

"You can call me Pedro."

"I'm glad you picked me, Pedro," she managed, although the words threatened to choke her.

"Why?" he asked.

Most men would have taken the compliment at face value. Now she scrambled for an answer. "Because it's an honor to be selected by a man who is so commanding."

He chuckled, the sound hardly pleasant. "I'm glad you approve."

"So where are you from?" she asked casually.

"That's none of your business."

"I—I was just trying to make conversation," she answered quickly.

"I don't need conversation. I want sex. I haven't had a

woman in months," he announced, then began to unbutton
his shirt.

Oh great, she thought. Was he going to give her time to
get the drug onto his skin? Or was he in too much of a
hurry to get to the main event? How could she slow him
down? A drink? She moved toward the side table that was
set up like a small bar.

Since she'd arrived at the McDonough Club, she'd been
in some sticky situations in this room. But she knew without doubt that this man was the most dangerous john she'd
taken up here, and she couldn't afford to make any mistake
with him.

Before she could offer him a drink, his tongue flicked
across his lips, and her attention was drawn to that greedy
gesture. Then she raised her gaze to his eyes. He was
watching her as he undid the buttons of his shirt, and she
saw that his chest was a mass of healed scars, like someone
had whipped him repeatedly.

It took all her resolve not to back away. Then she
couldn't contain a strangled noise when more scarred skin
was revealed, and she saw something else—an ominous-
looking tattoo.

He caught the small noise and his busy hands stopped
moving on the buttons. "You don't like my scars?" he
asked, a dangerous edge in his voice, and she knew that he
wasn't a man who was comfortable with his body.

She swallowed. "That's not for me to judge."

"I think you *are* judging, *Señorita* Gillian, whether you
admit it or not. I think you don't like being in this bedroom
with me."

"That's not true," she said weakly, wishing he couldn't
read her quite so well.

He studied her intently. "I could make your face look

like my chest,'' he said, the words low and cutting, like a knife digging into her flesh.

She couldn't stop herself from gasping. When she saw his gaze intensify, she knew he enjoyed her reaction.

Gillian went very still. This dark and dangerous hombre was nothing like the other johns she had duped since she'd come to the McDonough Club. He was used to getting what he wanted—with no questions asked.

"I mean no offense, *Señor* Pedro," she said. "A scarred body turns me on."

He gave her a nasty sneer. "So you say. But that's not what your eyes told me. I caught your look of distaste when you saw the lines on my skin," he said, his voice low and menacing, his gaze narrowed as he studied her.

A moment ago she'd thought he was dangerous. He'd just turned up the menace meter a hundred degrees.

Gillian knew she could be in serious trouble. The tone of his voice told her she was walking a tightrope. What if she pressed the panic button at the head of the bed? Would anyone come to her rescue? Or were honored guests excluded from safety considerations? Was that why a girl had gotten hurt the last time?

Thinking she'd be better off handling him on her own, she tried another tack. "It wasn't the scars," she said carefully. "I was wondering about that scorpion tattoo on your chest."

The moment the words were out of her mouth, she knew from the way his eyes narrowed that she'd made a major mistake.

Chapter Eleven

In the van both Alex and Rich sat with their attention riveted to the dialogue from Gillian's room.

"Well, I guess that confirms it," Alex muttered. "The scumbags from Nilia are the special group Madam Dupré was expecting."

"Yeah."

Alex clenched and unclenched his fist. "We could call in the cops to arrest the whole bunch of them right now!"

"For what? Patronizing a house of prostitution? Their lawyer would have them out in hours. They'd be mad as a river full of piranhas. And they'd know that something's up. We'd have to pull Gillian out of there and put her in a safe house."

Alex answered with a curse, even when his brain knew that Rich was right.

His attention snapped back to the conversation as the man asked in a deadly calm voice, "What about the scorpion?"

"It's an unusual choice for a tattoo," Gillian said, obviously speaking carefully. "How did you happen to get it?"

Almost as soon as the words were out of her mouth, the sound of a hand striking flesh rang out.

Gillian whimpered, and Alex cursed again. The bastard had slapped her just for asking about the damn tattoo. It felt like the blow had landed on his own face, and he struggled to catch his breath.

The man's angry voice was the next thing they heard. *"Puta,* you do not question me about my private business. The only thing you need to know is how to pleasure me."

Alex shifted in his seat. His stomach was tied in knots and his chest was so tight that he could hardly breathe.

"Yes," Gillian answered in a voice that she couldn't quite hold steady.

"When you answer me, you say, '*Sí, señor.*'"

"Sí, señor," she echoed, the quaver still in her voice.

Somehow that quaver was the last straw for Alex. He was already out of his chair and halfway across the van before the words were out of her mouth.

"Wait," Rich called. "You can't just go charging in there. What are you going to do?"

"I did it before. I can do it again." He flung the words over his shoulder as he yanked open the door of the van and charged up the street toward the McDonough Club.

THE DOOR OF THE BEDROOM opened with a snap. Gillian felt a mixture of relief and astonishment as Alex stepped inside. He was wearing a white dress shirt and dark slacks. Turning carefully, he closed the barrier behind him.

At the sound of the interruption, the man named Pedro whirled and before Gillian could blink, had reached toward his ankle and pulled a small pistol from under his pant leg.

Gillian had been frightened for herself. When she saw that gun pointed at Alex's chest, her mouth went dry as baked mud. It was a small caliber revolver, but at close range she knew it could do considerable damage. Somehow she managed to speak. "Don't do anything foolish, *señor.*"

She might as well have been inaudible and invisible, because all of the man's considerable attention was focused on Alex.

"Who are you?" the thug demanded.

"A satisfied customer," Alex answered, sounding surprisingly calm considering the deadly circumstances. Spreading his hands to show that they were empty, he continued in the same even tone. "The woman is right. You don't want to get arrested for murder." As he spoke, his gaze flicked from the gun to Gillian and back again.

The thug raised his chin. "Nobody would dare arrest me here," he said, but his voice was one beat less sure than it had been a moment ago when he'd pulled the weapon.

"I think there's been a small mistake," Alex said. "But we can easily fix it."

"What mistake?" the bad hombre asked.

"I had an appointment with this woman. I've been with her before, and I've been looking forward all week to being with her again. I didn't expect to find someone else in her room. I'm sorry I interrupted your pleasure," he added in a consolatory voice.

There was a charged moment when both men stood tensely facing each other. Then Pedro apparently realized the wisdom of ratcheting the tension down a notch, because he shoved his gun into the waistband of his slacks. "I'm here now," he said. "You can find someone else."

"I selected this woman," Alex said.

"So did I."

"But I have the first priority," Alex said, keeping his voice even but firm. "I'm sorry that she was asked to come downstairs."

Gillian wanted to speak but kept her lips pressed together because she knew that Pedro didn't give a damn about her opinion.

"This house is full of beautiful and talented women who would love to perform any act that your very imaginative mind can conjure up. You can easily find another willing partner," Alex said.

It appeared that Pedro was considering the words. Probably he was weighing what it was worth to make a stink about one particular prostitute. She wanted to tell him that he wouldn't lose face by finding another bed partner, but she was pretty sure that if she made the observation, he'd do just the opposite. So she kept silent.

Her heart banged around inside her chest as she waited for Pedro to make his decision. Finally he buttoned up his shirt, then gave Gillian one last malevolent look.

"The bitch talks too much. You're welcome to her. But you may have to teach her better manners," he growled as he brushed past Alex. Exiting the room, he slammed the door behind him.

Alex swiftly crossed the carpet and caught Gillian in his arms. With a little sob, she melted against him.

Just one, sharp sob. She'd managed to cope with the men who came to this room with her. But with Pedro, she'd known she was over her head.

Alex had been in the van, listening. He'd known she was in trouble and he'd come to her rescue.

She should push herself away from him. She should act like she was perfectly fine. Instead she closed her eyes as his hands soothed over her back and shoulders, calming her. To her horror, she felt herself shaking and couldn't stop.

"It's okay."

She gulped. "I screwed up."

"How?"

"I said something about his tattoo."

"There was no way you could win. It was either the scars

or the tattoo. And if you hadn't answered the question, he would have slapped you around for defying him.''

"I..."

"Shh," he soothed. "Don't beat yourself up." He brushed his lips against her cheek, then loosened his hold on her.

She didn't want to be alone now. Panic leaped inside her chest, until she realized he wasn't going to let her go. He was only locking the door—which was a good idea, considering the way the maid had come bursting in on them the last time they'd been together here. And considering she'd been so off balance that she hadn't even thought about that with Pedro.

He ushered her back across the room, so that the two of them were standing near the window.

"Did you see the scorpion on his chest?" she asked.

"Yes. And I heard you."

She nodded.

"Let me talk to Rich for a minute," he said, then addressed the other agent in the van. "Stay on post. Get whoever's on backup tonight to watch the door. I want to know where Pedro goes when he leaves the club."

There was no answer, but she had to assume that the other man had gotten the message, since Alex had obviously heard loud and clear what was going on in this room.

She watched the expression on his face carefully. "You want to follow him, don't you?" she asked.

"We don't know when he's leaving. And I want to stay here with you."

"But?" she pressed.

"I just remembered the backup guy tonight is Mason Bartley."

She tipped her head to one side. "You don't think he can handle the assignment?"

"I'd like someone more reliable."

"Then go back out to the van and make some alternate arrangements. You don't have to baby-sit me," she said quickly because she didn't want any special favors.

"You're forgetting that I have to stay here for a while, since I made a big deal of wanting to screw you tonight," he snapped.

PEDRO RODRIGUEZ PAUSED on the landing. With an effort, he controlled his features before descending the stairs. He was damned if he was going to let anyone know he had backed down.

There were still a few *putas* in the parlor—the stragglers nobody had chosen, he thought with a scornful look. The man who had lined the merchandise up was gone, but the madam came hurrying forward when she saw him standing in the doorway. He took a moment to enjoy her discomfort.

"*Señor?* Is there some problem?" she asked.

He shrugged elaborately. "Another man came in. He claimed that the girl named Gillian was already promised to him."

"Gillian? Another man is with her?"

"*Sí,*" Pedro snapped. "This is supposed to be a high-class house. She should be more careful about her schedule," he said.

"I'll certainly dock her pay," the woman said.

Pedro nodded in satisfaction. "She's too full of herself. You should whip some humility into her."

He saw the women still in the room listening avidly, although most of them were pretending they hadn't heard a thing. One of them, a redhead, nodded in agreement.

The madam made a sound that might have also been agreement. He hoped so. "Keep an eye on her," he advised, knowing he was getting her into trouble.

"I certainly will. I'm so sorry about the mix-up," the madam said. "How can I make it up to you?"

His gaze flicked to the remaining whores. But he could see they were all ears. "You can make it up to me by giving me two of the others for my pleasure," he suggested. "That should be more fun than having the stupid one for a bed partner."

"Of course. That's an excellent suggestion," the woman approved quickly, probably relieved that she'd gotten off so easily.

"I want the redhead," he said, looking at the girl who had been so interested in the conversation. "And the brunette."

"Certainly." She motioned to the girls, and they hurried over.

"Our guest wants both of you to entertain him."

"Oh, that sounds like fun," the redhead murmured, looking from him to her colleague and back again. "Let's all go up to my room and get comfortable."

The brunette nodded. "Yes. Let's go. I'm Lisa and this is Babs. We make a very good team. You'll love what the two of us can do for you."

"Bueno."

The brunette gave him a knowing smile, a smile that made him start getting hard.

He let her lead him to the steps, his hand caressing her ass as she preceded him, squeezing a little bit hard to see how she'd react. She wiggled herself against his palm, and he decided that this was going to work out after all, especially when the whore in back of him started playing with *his* ass. He only scowled once, when he caught sight of the closed door where the guy was inside with the nosy bitch.

He jerked his head toward the door. "You know that girl, Gillian?" he asked.

"Yes," the one in back of him muttered, and from the sound of her voice, he knew the two of them weren't friends.

Keeping his own tone even, he said, "She's trouble. And that guy with her."

"You're right about that," the whore said, her voice low and nasty, and he had the feeling she would jump at the chance to get even with Gillian for some slight he didn't know about. She'd given him an idea, a very good idea.

GILLIAN LOOKED AWAY from Alex, her posture stiff, and he was instantly sorry that he'd spoken harshly to her.

"I didn't mean to snap at you," he said. "I'm on edge. We both are."

When she remained silent, he added, "I mean, we're both trying to get through a damn nasty assignment the best we can."

She started to take a step back. Before she could escape, he put one hand on her shoulder. With the other, he tipped up her chin so he could inspect the cheek that Pedro had slapped. His fingers had also caught the edge of her eye. "The bastard hurt you."

"I'm okay," she said in a thin voice. "You should leave."

She was trying to act tough, but he knew she was still shaking inside.

Clearing his throat, he said, "You're going to have a bruise if you don't get some ice on that."

When she gave a small nod, he turned her loose and strode to the bathroom where he retrieved a hand towel. Next he crossed to the small bar and opened the ice bucket that sat next to several bottles of whiskey, soda and the pitcher of fresh orange juice, which were available to guests.

"Lie down," he directed as he made a compress of towel and ice cubes. Then, because he wanted to be alone with her, he turned off the lipstick microphone.

Gillian lay down on the bed and he eased onto the mattress beside her. Gently he positioned the towel over her cheek and the edge of her eye.

Gillian rested there with her eyes closed for a few moments. Then the eyelid he could see snapped open again.

"He looks like he's ruled by his emotions. Pedro, I mean. But he's smart," she said.

"Because he chose not to blow me away?"

"Yes, thank God." She'd kept her arms at her sides. Now she reached for his hand and knit her fingers with his. "Alex, you were taking a chance coming in here like that."

"He hurt you once. I didn't want to find out what else he was going to do behind your closed door."

"Thank you," she whispered.

"You would have done the same thing if I were in trouble," he said, his voice gruff.

"Yes," she answered without hesitation, then dragged in a breath and let it out in a rush. "I should have gotten more information from him."

"Too dangerous," he snapped. "Look what happened when you mentioned his tattoo."

She answered with a tight nod.

Alex opened his mouth to speak, but she pressed her fingers against his lips. He knew she'd been struggling not to show him any vulnerability. Now she whispered the first request she'd made since he'd come into the room.

"Just hold me," she said.

CYNTHIA DUPRÉ LOOKED at the two girls still in the parlor. Really, she should stay in case any customers came in. But there was something important she had to do. "I'll be in my office. Let me know if any more guests arrive," she said.

"Yes, ma'am," Sandra answered.

After another moment's hesitation, she left the public area of the club and headed down the hall. Gaspard had inspected the food and the liquor. Thank the Lord he had approved of her choices and left when the men had gone upstairs. Apparently he was satisfied with the way the evening was going.

But sometimes he had a habit of popping back in to see how things were running. Well, she'd just have to take a chance that he wasn't coming back any time soon.

First she picked up the appointment book where the girls made note of any dates they'd made. Then she headed for her office.

Stepping into the comfortably decorated space, she carried the book to her desk, sat down and flipped to the day's appointments.

Gillian Stanwick had listed nothing for that evening. Had she made a date with a customer and forgotten to write it down? Which was why the man upstairs with Gillian assumed she'd be free? Or did they have some kind of private arrangement? That would certainly never do.

Marching to the bookcase, Cynthia activated the monitors.

At the present, she saw scenes of various girls with the Latin American men who had come here as a special treat paid for by a benefactor in the city.

It was tempting to take a peek—or a longer look—at what was going on. One of the ways she amused herself was to watch the various sexual acts being performed upstairs. Well, it wasn't just for fun, she added quickly. By watching the girls, she was able to tell who was good at what and whether they were giving the customers their money's worth. And she was also able to check on various complaints.

But now there was only one complaint that concerned her. Frank had told her the camera in room eight had been fixed that morning. So she switched to the view in Gillian's room.

When the picture flopped up and down, she bit out a curse.

"Now what?" she fumed.

Yet she knew she was looking at a picture of Gillian Stanwick and a man lying on her bed.

Reaching for the horizontal hold, she stabilized the picture and leaned forward, trying to assess exactly what was going on in the bedroom—a prostitute servicing a john or a private tryst with a special friend bold and brash enough to interrupt a whore with an important customer?

A SMALL BUZZING SOUND barely registered at the edge of Alex's consciousness. It might have been from a fly trapped in the room. But when he felt Gillian stiffen, he realized she knew something he didn't.

"What?" he murmured.

She lowered her mouth to his ear as though she were nuzzling him. "That's the sound of the camera coming on," she whispered.

Alex froze. "Where?" he asked in a gruff voice, figuring that the question wouldn't give too much away even if someone heard what he was saying.

"In the frame of the picture. Over by the armoire," she replied, the words barely audible.

He turned his back to the large piece of furniture. Rearing over her, he blocked the view from across the room, then carefully whispered another question, "Didn't you use that equipment we gave you to turn it off?"

"Of course," she breathed. "I keep doing that. And they keep coming in and fixing it. I was sure it was still disabled. I guess Frank got to it while I was out."

He considered who might be watching and what they might be seeing. A man and a woman on a bed. But they weren't doing much yet.

"Okay," he practically mouthed the word, adding, "Then we'd better make this look good."

Panic bloomed on her face.

"Relax. You're in good hands," he whispered, then moved to the side to provide a view of Gillian's body as he began slowly undoing the buttons that closed the front of her dress. He tried to do it smoothly, but the sudden tension had made his fingers clumsy.

Gillian lay there on the bed, looking up at him questioningly, and he hoped she didn't know how badly his nerves were jumping.

He bent his head, pretending to be absorbed in the job of unfastening the dress. But his mind was spinning. The camera had been turned off until a few minutes ago, but now somebody was curious about the present occupants of the room. Probably because that hulking bastard Pedro had charged directly from Gillian's room and complained to the madam when he hadn't gotten satisfied.

Well, Alex should have been expecting that. Only he'd been too wound up with Gillian to be considering anything going on outside the room.

He kept sliding buttons open, unfastening the dress all the way to the hemline, telling himself that they had to make this look like what the watcher expected to see. But really, most of his attention was focused on the woman who lay on the bed with her arms at her sides and her eyes dark and heavy-lidded as they regarded him.

Her bra and panties were modest, yet sexy-looking at the

same time. Unable to stop himself, he stroked the opening he'd made, dragging his hand slowly along her skin, stopping to dip his finger under the edge of her bra, then reaching down to draw little circles on her abdomen.

Her breath turned shaky, making him want to go further. Much further. All he had to do to bare her breasts was adjust the cups of her bra.

He shifted so he was blocking the camera's view, then folded down the cups, revealing the hidden treasures beneath.

"Beautiful," he murmured, stroking the silken curves he'd uncovered, then moving one hand back and forth between her nipples, feeling them harden enticingly under his fingers.

Despite the circumstances, she was aroused, and that fueled his own passion. It felt like he had wanted to make love to Gillian forever. And now here she was, in his arms, on a bed.

She made a small, needy sound, asking for more. Glad to oblige, he bent his head, still blocking the camera's view as he swirled his tongue around one of those hardened tips, then taking it gently in his teeth, before sucking it into his mouth. The texture was wonderful. And when she arched into the caress, he pressed his erection against her thigh.

Her hand reached to find the buttons on his shirt, opening some so that she could slip her fingers inside and run them through the hair on his chest, her touch turning him molten.

So much blood had drained from his brain that he was rapidly losing the ability to think. Except to wonder how he had managed to walk away from this woman two years ago. He would go mad if he didn't make love to her now. And he sure as hell wasn't going to do it in front of an audience.

"Come on," he insisted.

Her eyes blinked open and she stared at him as though she'd just surfaced from twenty thousand fathoms. "Where?"

He wasn't sure what he'd been going to say. But he heard himself coming up with an interesting story. "I'm hot and sweaty, and I didn't get a chance to shower before I came here. I'd like you to do that for me."

She opened her mouth, then closed it again.

Standing, he reached for her hand, then pulled her off the bed and led her across the rug to the bathroom.

"Privacy," he growled as he closed the door.

"What about…about…?"

Marching to the tub, he turned on the shower. "The water will block out the microphone in the other room," he said over his shoulder.

Reaching for her again, he swept the dress off her shoulders and threw it onto the black-and-white-tiled floor before folding her into his arms. Lowering his head, he covered her mouth with his.

The kiss blazed white-hot between them, born of frustration and fear and need. They might be in big trouble, but all he could think about was devouring her mouth, even as she helped him tear off his clothing. By the time they were both naked, the room was rapidly filling with steam and his erection was jutting out from his body like a telephone pole.

Turning to the shower, he left the water running but adjusted the temperature so that the atmosphere in the bathroom was a little more bearable. Then he closed the toilet seat with a thump, sat down on the cover, and reached for Gillian again. She came willingly, eagerly standing with her legs on either side of the seat as she leaned over him, sensuously caressing his back and shoulders, kissing the side of his face and brow.

He played with her breasts, kissing and touching them

with one hand as the other slid down her body to find the hidden, feminine core of her.

"Oh, Alex," she sobbed as he touched her there, then quickly bent her knees.

They both exclaimed something incoherent as her hot, tight channel closed around him. He reached to clasp her to him, holding her still for a long moment, reveling in the feel of her body clasping his. But that wasn't enough. Not nearly enough.

"Let me," she breathed.

"Oh yes."

She rocked her body over his, up and down, as they exchanged more scorching kisses.

When he began to caress her breasts again, she called out his name, her movements becoming more frantic by the second.

Gigantic rolling waves of emotion and physical sensations swept them to a quick, shattering climax. She collapsed against him, her head on his shoulder, and he stroked the damp skin of her back. It had been a wild, all-consuming ride. But it had been over much too quickly.

"Oh, Alex," she murmured, gathering him close. "Alex." Her voice broke as she said his name the second time.

He kissed her cheek, the edge of her hair. For long moments neither of them moved.

He wanted to stay close to her forever. The thought of getting dressed and walking out the door made his chest tighten painfully. How much more time could he spend with her? Half an hour? Less?

It was impossible to get up and walk away. Not yet.

"I think I owe you a shower," he finally said, because that would delay his departure.

She nodded, then stood and backed away, blinking as

though she couldn't believe where they were and what they had just done.

Clasping her hand, he led her across the cold tile to the tub. They both climbed in, and he pulled the curtain, locking them away from the world as they stood, holding each other under the pounding water.

SHE STROKED her hands over the wet skin of his back, down his hips, sealing him to her, and he felt himself getting hard again. They stood together for long moments before she murmured, "We're going to use up all the hot water in the house."

"We're entitled to some privileges," he answered as he reached for the soap and lathered his hands, then ran them down her neck, over her shoulders and onto her breasts. The water and the soap made his hands slick, so that they glided sensuously over her breasts, then her bottom. She made a low purring sound as his slickened hands moved over her. Then she was reaching for the soap and working up her own lather. When her hand closed around his erection and began a slow, sliding motion, he dragged in a shaky breath.

"That feels so good," she breathed.

"Yeah." He laughed. "At this end, too."

She laughed with him.

"But maybe too good. I want to be inside you for the second round."

"Here? In the shower?"

Instead of answering, he covered her mouth with his. Then he washed the soap from his hands and body and reached between her legs, finding the hot, swollen core of her. Bracing his back against the wall, he lifted her up and entered her, then moved her hips in a slow, steady rhythm that soon became more frantic. She hung on to him, bracing her feet against the high edge of the tub. And they climbed toward another shattering climax.

The water temperature had dropped considerably by the time he shut off the faucets.

Pulling a towel from the rack, he tenderly dried Gillian's body, then worked on her hair.

"I need to use the dryer and brush it," she murmured.

He turned her loose, watching her slip into a robe, then work on her hair as he dried himself and reached for his underwear.

When he was dressed, he turned to her. "Are you going to get in trouble?"

"Because of Pedro? I don't know."

"Him, maybe. But I also stayed over an hour. You've probably got a time limit with johns."

When she winced, he wished he'd thought of a more delicate way to say it.

"You can offer to pay Madam Dupré extra. That should take care of the overtime problem," she said in a clipped voice.

He gave her an appraising look. A few minutes ago they'd been very close. Now it sounded like she was trying to put some distance between them.

"What about the Pedro problem?" he asked carefully.

"I guess I'll have to deal with it, won't I?"

There were a lot of things he might have said. He settled for, "I don't like leaving you here."

"But you will," she said tightly. "Because we both have a job to do. Like, we've got to find out why the men you've been tracking ended up in the McDonough Club, of all places.

He wanted to argue with her. Instead he gave a tight nod and left.

The only thing that gave him the strength to walk out on her was that old game he played with himself—the game where he thought of all the reasons why he should stay away from her. All the reasons why his damn abnormal upbringing made him a bad risk for relationships.

This time he summoned up a doozy. The time when he'd been fifteen and Flora, the woman his dad was going with, had come on to Alex. They'd been alone in the kitchen. Dad had gone out to pick up Chinese carryout, and she'd pressed her hand against the fly of his jeans. He'd been embarrassed. And turned on. He hadn't known how to handle the situation. So he'd told her to tell his dad he was going to a friend's house. And he'd fled, hearing her laughter follow him down the block.

He fled now because he was stuck in another situation he didn't know how to handle. Only this time it was different. A lot different.

But he couldn't let his personal feelings get in the way. They'd have to stay on hold until the case was wrapped up.

Chapter Twelve

"Where's Mason Bartley's report?" Alex demanded. He was standing in the New Orleans Confidential office, with his hands fisted on his hips, trying not to jump down Seth Lewis's throat.

Conrad Burke had taken several hours of personal leave that morning. Apparently his twins had sore throats and he'd been drafted by his wife, Marilyn, to help take them to the doctor.

Because Seth had no present outside assignment, he had been left in charge of the office and he was having trouble locating all of the files he needed on Conrad's less than tidy desk.

"Bartley was supposed to follow that guy Pedro," Alex said impatiently. "Where did he go?"

Seth scrabbled through papers and read several lines of text. "His report says he lost him."

"What?" Alex shouted.

"I'm only delivering the information," Seth said calmly.

Alex shifted his weight from one foot to the other. "Sorry," he muttered. "Let me see the report."

Seth handed it across the desk. Alex read rapidly, then swore. "He got behind him in traffic. Then the light changed. Some super-sleuth he is!"

"Yeah."

"Our best lead in the investigation and he lost him."

"Yeah."

"Do you think Bartley's really on our side?" Alex asked in a low voice. "Or is he being paid by the opposition? I mean, what has he done right since he joined this organization?"

"I guess you'll have to take that up with Conrad Burke."

Alex nodded tightly.

"There's something else that might interest you," Seth offered.

"Like what?"

"Like, Sebastion Primeaux asked for a report on the Category Five case."

Alex's brows shot up. "The district attorney? How does he even know about it? The operation is supposed to be secret."

"He has his ways of keeping current on everything that's going on in town. Burke had me do a background report on him." He cleared his throat. "Probably you haven't had a chance to read it, since you've been busy in the surveillance van, so I can fill you in, if you want," Seth finished, being careful not to imply that Alex should be keeping himself up to speed on all aspects of the case.

"Yeah, go ahead," Alex said. Truthfully, he'd been so focused on watching over Gillian that he'd neglected to do his homework on some other details.

"To be brief, he's a bad combination—very powerful and very corrupt."

"How does a guy like that hold on to the job of district attorney?" Alex asked.

"Well, he has a lot of influential people in his corner because he's smart and careful. He looks, acts and speaks the politically correct way to keep the powers that be happy, but in reality he's as slimy as a used car salesman.''

''Just great!'' Alex muttered.

''He's more than willing to bend—or rather break—the rules to further his own agenda. Dig below the surface and you find that bribery, extortion and tax fraud are his way of life. And one more thing that might interest you. Nobody would speak on the record about his sexual preferences, but I heard some talk that he likes to bonk underage prostitutes.''

That last statement caught Alex's interest as he thought back over what Gillian had told him. She'd said there were teenage girls being forced to work in the McDonough Club. She'd even seen a man requesting the services of one of them. A man who spoke with a courtly New Orleans drawl. ''Do you have a picture of the scumbag?'' he asked Seth.

The other agent shuffled through a folder and brought out a black-and-white five-by-seven head shot of a smiling man, obviously meant as a publicity photo. He looked to be in his mid-fifties, with slicked-back brown hair, brown eyes and some gray at his temples.

''What do you want with the photograph?''

''It might come in handy,'' he said, thinking that maybe he could use the photo as an excuse for going back to Gillian.

The phone rang and Seth answered. ''Yes, Chief Courville,'' he said. ''No, I'm sorry, Conrad Burke is not available at the moment.''

Alex knew he was taking to the chief of police. And the scowl on his face told him it wasn't good news.

GILLIAN HAD ENDURED a dressing-down from Madam Dupré that morning. She'd had to explain over and over that Alex was a legitimate john. Still, she'd had her wages docked for the rest of the month. And she knew she was in danger of being fired over the supposed mix-up in her schedule. But somehow she'd talked her way back into the madam's good graces. Maybe because Madam Dupré was determined to show Gaspard that she hadn't made a serious mistake in hiring her. Apparently nobody had told him about the mix-up last night, and Gillian fervently hoped he never heard about it.

What's more, she was taking an even bigger chance than usual, she silently acknowledged, as she made her way down the hall to the part of the house that was technically off-limits. But since she'd learned about the teenagers being held as virtual captives, she'd felt compelled to come back again and again to see if she could help any of them. Maybe it was because she kept thinking about her own family. They were close, and when her cousin Maggie had run away, Uncle Fritz and Aunt Mary had been devastated. Maggie had eventually called her mom and dad and asked to come back home. But Gillian shuddered to think about what might have happened to her if she'd been scooped up by someone like Gaspard.

She stopped short when she heard voices behind one of the closed doors. Frank was speaking harshly to a kid who obviously didn't want to be there.

"Just let me leave, okay? I'll go home. I won't give my…family…any more trouble."

"I'm afraid I can't let you go, missy. You came here of your own free will, and now you have to deal with it."

"No, I didn't! Just let me go," the girl repeated.

"Monsieur Gaspard is busy right now. He'll be back to talk to you soon. So don't get your knickers in a twist."

How soon? Gillian wondered. How much time did she have?

She watched Frank step into the hall, lock the door behind him and stride down the corridor. Quickly, before she got caught, she hurried to the door and she snapped the lock open.

When she stepped inside, she saw a scruffy-looking teenage girl huddled on the sofa. She looked up in terror as Gillian entered the room.

"No, please," she whimpered.

"I'm not going to hurt you. I want to help you," Gillian said.

"How do I know you're telling the truth?" the girl asked in a shaky voice. "How do I know you're not going to trick me—the way *he* tricked me into coming here?"

"I guess you have to trust me. What's your name?"

"Lily."

"Okay, Lily. If you get out of here, what are you going to do? Go back on the street?"

"I just want to get in touch with my father. If I can get away from this place."

"I'll help you," Gillian said.

Before she could say more, the sound of footsteps approaching the room made her freeze. "I can't do it now. But I promise I won't abandon you," she whispered, diving into the closet.

Through the slit in the door, she saw Frank.

"Come on," he said gruffly. The girl glanced toward the closet, and Gillian waited with the breath frozen in her lungs to find out if she was going to blab.

But she said nothing. Looking sick and scared, she let Frank lead her into the hall.

Feeling like she'd betrayed the girl, Gillian waited several minutes, then slipped back into the hall. She wouldn't let her promise turn into a lie. She'd find that kid and get her out of here, she vowed. But she couldn't do it now.

Before anyone caught sight of her loitering on the first floor, she made for the back stairs, then up to her room.

As soon as she was alone, she went into the bathroom to get out the special equipment that disabled the camera and checked on its status. She'd turned it off that morning. According to the readings, it was still off. So she walked to the window and spoke as she looked out into the sunlit street.

"I made contact with one of those runaway girls that Gaspard brings here. I tried to help her get away. But Frank came back," she said, because she had to tell someone what had happened.

She pictured Alex in the van—looking disapproving. He'd tell her it wasn't her job to get anybody out of the house. And really, she knew she'd jeopardized her position here. But she had to do it, because the idea of unsuspecting girls being brought here and forced to service slimeball guys turned her stomach. And if she'd made a difference for just one of them, then that was one less kid who was suffering the tortures of the damned.

BABS WAS ON HER WAY downstairs when she saw the man standing in the doorway—and froze.

It was *him.* The guy who had come swaggering in and claimed that he'd had an appointment with Gillian. Which was a bald-faced lie, of course. She'd been on call like everyone else to entertain those badass Latin American hombres.

And here was the dude back again, before they were really open for business, like he didn't know the girls had free time in the late afternoon.

She half turned and fiddled with a little dish on the table, peering at him from under lowered lashes. Maybe he thought he looked different. His hair was a lighter color.

And he was dressed in a business suit tonight and carried a leather briefcase. But Babs knew him, all right. She'd seen him charge upstairs. She knew he'd barged in on Gillian and Pedro, an account of which Pedro had given her in great detail, although she suspected the Latin guy was making it sound like he'd come off better than he actually had.

But the whole thing had ended up working out okay for her and Lisa.

In fact, it had been more than okay. Pedro had liked the way they had treated him. He'd given them a big tip. And he'd given Babs something even better. A white powder that said would make whoever you gave it to crazy horny. She might not have believed him, except that it sounded like the same stuff that Dolly and some of the other girls were whispering about. The way Dolly told it, a bartender would give it to the unsuspecting customers, then send them back here with Dolly or a few other girls.

Dolly had said it made them hot to trot, all right. It also made some of them sick. Some guys had ended up in the hospital and some had even died. At least, that's what she'd heard.

Babs had been thinking about slipping it into Gillian's drink and watching the fun. Maybe tonight would be a good night to do it. Maybe it would make her toss her cookies when her special friend was here.

She walked toward the guy, and his head jerked up. A smile split his face. In the next second, it was replaced by disappointment. She knew what had happened. He'd seen her red hair, and for a second he'd thought she was Gillian. Then he'd realized it wasn't her.

Well, too bad for him.

She'd fix him. With some of that powder.

Before he could say anything, she turned and went to

the bar. The powder was in the little evening purse that she liked to carry. Keeping her back to him, she fixed him a Planter's Punch, dropped in a nice big dose of the powder, and brought the drink across the room.

"Let me offer you a complimentary beverage," she said.

He looked surprised, but he took the drink. "I know it's early. But I was hoping to see Gillian," he said.

"Yes, it's early. Why don't you have a seat?"

He sat down on one of the armchairs and took a swallow of the drink.

She sat down beside him. "What's your name, handsome?"

"Alex," he answered.

"Are you staying long in town?" she asked, pretending she hadn't seen him the night before.

"Uh, I get here from time to time."

"Make yourself comfortable. This is your lucky night."

"What?" he asked, not getting the joke, of course. Well, he'd get it later.

She gave him a little smile. "I'll go see if Gillian is available."

When he took another swallow of the drink, she smiled at him and headed for the stairs, giving him a nice view of her swaying ass as she went.

IT SEEMED HOTTER in the room than it had a few minutes earlier. To cool himself, Alex took another swallow of the drink, then clasped the tumbler in his hand, letting the icy glass soothe his skin. He didn't usually go for mixed drinks. But this stuff tasted good, so he took another swallow.

He wouldn't be here now, except that he had a lot to discuss with Gillian. More than just the picture of the district attorney. Something that she had to know right away.

He was feeling kind of strange. Horny, actually. And a

broad smile plastered itself on his face as he thought about the lucky fact that a whorehouse was the perfect place for his present state.

By the time he saw Gillian come down the stairs, he was feeling a little light-headed. She wavered in his vision as she walked toward him, looking surprised and then alarmed as he mopped a sleeve of his jacket over his sweating brow.

"Alex?" she said.

The other red-haired woman was standing in the doorway, watching them.

"I thought I'd come back to see you," he said. "I thought we'd just have a nice intimate chat. But now..." He let his voice trail off suggestively, because he knew he was talking pretty loud. And maybe this wasn't the best place to discuss their private business.

Gillian stared at his face, then at the drink in his hand. "Where did you get that?" she asked carefully.

He raised the glass toward the other redhead, the one named Babs. "Your friend was kind enough to fix it for me."

Gillian turned toward the other woman. "Babs, what did you put in that drink?" she demanded.

Babs? Hadn't she mentioned Babs? What had she said about her?

The other woman shrugged, but the nasty look that flashed across her features sent a sizzle of alarm along his nerve endings. He stared at the glass in his hand, aware that he'd swallowed at least half the contents.

"Come up to my room," Gillian said.

"I should go," he said, partly because he could no longer remember why he had come.

Just to have sex with Gillian? He was so hard now, he was in pain. Sex. Yeah. But was there some other reason he'd come here?

He stood up and the room spun. If Gillian hadn't grabbed his arm, he would have ended up sprawled on his face. "Sorry," he muttered.

"Come up," she said again, and he had the panicked feeling that he should get away from her.

Yet he could feel her fingers burning his flesh through the fabric of his jacket and shirt, her touch so arousing that he could hardly breathe. And when she pried the glass from his fingers and set it down, he felt like she'd taken away his lifeline. "Wait a minute," he protested.

"Come on." She tugged on his arm, leading him toward the stairs. He followed.

Gillian was wearing a simple silky dress. He stroked his hand over her bottom, then up along the side of her breast. Questing inward, he trailed his fingers back and forth across the tip, gratified when he felt her nipple bead. Maybe she was as aroused as he was.

She shot him a startled look, and he realized they were still on the stairs where anyone could see them. But hell, you didn't exactly have to adhere to strict standards of decorum here.

The stuffy phrase made him laugh.

"What?" she demanded.

"Standards of decorum. You don't have to worry about standards of decorum in a whorehouse, do you?" He laughed again, enjoying the joke.

His cock was jammed against the front of his slacks and he wanted to unzip his fly. But probably that was going a little too far. Probably he should wait until he got into Gillian's room. But there was nothing wrong with nuzzling his lips against her neck or sucking the edge of her ear into his mouth.

"You taste good," he murmured.

She made what could have been a disapproving noise.

But he ignored her because they were almost at her room. Number eight.

"Behind the eight ball," he said, laughing again.

"Mmm, hmm," she answered, steering him inside and locking the door behind them.

He made it across the room, paused to kick off his loafers, then flopped onto the bed, where he lay grinning at her.

Hearing something thunk to the floor, he looked over the side of the bed.

"Where did you get my briefcase?" he asked.

"I brought it up," she answered.

"I forgot all about it," he muttered. "We have to talk about something important."

"What?"

"I don't remember." He worried about that for five seconds. Then his mind drifted to another topic. He was thinking that he could always hold his liquor. But not this afternoon.

"I'm drunk as a skunk. And I only had half a glass of Planter's Punch."

"I know," she said in a low voice as she turned off the microphone that broadcast to the van.

"Don't get mad at me," he said. "It's not my fault."

"I know," she answered again, and the tone of her voice made him struggle to focus on her.

"Don't be mad," he said again, pulling her down beside him and nuzzling her again, giving her neck and the edge of her jaw sloppy kisses that were highly arousing.

"Take off your clothes," he said thickly. "Then take off mine," he added because the buttons on the front of his shirt were too difficult to manage.

When he started pawing at the front of her dress, she took both his hands in one of hers.

"Alex, listen to me," she said.

"I don't want to talk. I want to sc—"

Before he could finish the sentence, she pressed the fingers of her free hand over his lips.

"Alex, you have to listen to me," she said again. This time her tone was pleading, and he made an effort to focus on her words.

"Um?"

"Let me take your pulse."

"If that's what turns you on." That struck him as powerfully funny, and he couldn't stop laughing. With an effort, he lay still while she pressed her fingers to his wrist. He closed his eyes and drifted, tethered to her by her firm hold.

"It's very rapid. Your skin is flushed. You're perspiring. You…you're very aroused. You're acting like everything is a big joke." She gulped. "I think Babs drugged you," she whispered.

His eyes blinked open and he made an effort to focus on her. "Huh?"

"That drink that Babs gave you. I'm sure it was drugged."

He laughed again, because he knew she had to be joking. "No way!"

"With that Category Five stuff," she continued, ignoring his protest.

"No way," he said again, but a little worm of alarm was burrowing into his mind.

"We've been looking for the source in this house. We thought it was the bartender at Bourbon Street Libations who was giving it to customers. But it must be here, too. And Babs got her hands on a dose."

He shook his head, still trying to convince himself it wasn't true. But he felt damn weird. Like his brain and his vision were out of focus, and all he wanted to do was get into Gillian's pants.

He thought back to the night it had all started, at Bourbon Street Libations—and the way Wiley Longbottom had been acting.

"Damn," he muttered, then struggled to a sitting position. "I'd better get out of here. I could be dangerous."

She pushed him back onto the bed. "You're not in any shape to leave. I saw the police department report on guys who got Category Five."

Her words cut through the fog in his brain. "What the hell are you talking about? What reports?"

"We have interviews with men who were given the drug. And medical reports. We only got minimal information."

"I didn't see any reports." He cursed loudly. "Which means Courville didn't share what he knew with us," he growled.

"I...I'm sorry. I thought you had the same information we got. There were twenty-five or thirty interviews."

He had broken out in a hot sweat as he struggled to make his brain function. Deep in his mind he knew what he *should* do. He should leave. No. He couldn't leave. He had come here to talk to Gillian about something vital. But he couldn't remember what it was. Really, he was so aroused, he could barely think. There was room for only one basic idea. "I've got to tell my boss about those reports."

"Alex, you can't."

"What—are you trying to keep information from New Orleans Confidential?" he barked, wondering if he was sounding rational, even as he tried to hold on to his sanity.

Her fingers dug into his shoulder. Her other hand turned his face toward hers. Her gaze was fierce. "You have to listen to me. I *know* what happened to those guys. The one who gave in and let the drug work its way through their systems came out okay. The ones who tried to fight it ended up in the hospital. That must be what happened to Wiley Longbottom. He couldn't give in to the stuff.''

He swore again, trying to take in what she was saying, trying to figure out what he should do.

''Alex, let me help you.'' She pushed him gently back on to the bed and curled herself next to him as she covered his aching erection with her hand. When she rocked her palm against him, he gasped, feeling a jolt of sensation that was half pleasure and half pain.

All thought fled his mind. The only thing he knew for sure was that he was about to go off like a rocket. There was no time to get undressed. No time to even unzip his slacks. He pressed his hand over hers, grinding her palm and fingers against himself through two layers of fabric as he arched his hips. The effect was like throwing a match onto gasoline-soaked tinder. It took only seconds for his body to reach flash point. His muscles jerked and he gasped as the orgasm took him. The sensations came sharp and fast, leaving him sucking breath into his lungs as he flopped back against the pillows.

He was too spent to even curse. And too embarrassed to look Gillian in the eye. Talk about selfish, instant gratification!

He'd just embarrassed himself on so many levels that he couldn't even name them. And he knew damn well that he hadn't done a damn thing for her, although probably she wasn't feeling anything besides disgust at the moment. But at least he was capable of climbing off the bed. ''Okay,'' he managed to say. ''Let me get out of here. I have to talk to Burke.''

''No. You have to stay with me.''

His face was already flushed. He felt his cheeks go two shades hotter.

''Sorry,'' he mumbled. ''I guess I owe you....''

She took him by the shoulders and gave him a shake. "Alex, you don't owe me anything. But you can't leave," she answered. "I mean—you may feel okay right now. But it's not over. It's going to hit you again."

"God, no." But even as he uttered the denial, he felt his blood rising toward boiling point again. "You don't want to be in bed with me now," he choked out.

Gillian wrapped her arms around him. "Alex, let me be here for you. Let me help you through this."

"You should run like hell," he whispered. "Can't you see I'm out of control?"

"That's not your fault. Don't fight it. Let it happen. Maybe this time you can even take the time to enjoy it."

He still had a few brain cells functioning, enough to ask, "What about the camera? The last time I was here, there was somebody watching."

"I turned it off again. I'll know if they try to reactivate it."

"Good," he breathed, flopping back against the mattress, wondering if he could manage to give Gillian some pleasure out of this encounter.

He lay with his eyes closed for several moments. They snapped open again when he heard clothing rustling. He made a strangled sound when he saw what he had only known by touch earlier. She must have gotten dressed in a real rush because she was wearing nothing under her dress. And she looked so desirable and sexy that he wanted to eat her alive.

"Oh, Lord, Gillian."

Helpless to deny the need raging through him, he reached out and pulled her close again.

He needed to touch all the tender, feminine parts of her— her throat, her breasts, her belly, her hips. And he took a sensual tour of those treasures, trying to be gentle when his hands felt like blocks of wood.

When she raised up, he thought she was going to pull away. Instead she began working the buckle of his belt and then his zipper.

As she undressed him, he stroked between her legs, amazed that she was wet and slick.

"You want to make love with an out-of-control maniac?" he asked in a strangled voice.

"I want to make love with *you*," she answered, helping him pull off his pants, then tossing them onto the floor.

She rolled to her back and held out her arms. Helpless to ignore the invitation, he covered her body with his.

Her hand closed around him, then quickly guided him into her tight warmth.

His brain urged him to hold back, but his body had other ideas, and he exploded hard and fast again. Once more, he felt limp and exhausted. But he knew he must be a dead weight on top of her, so he tried to flop to his side.

"Stay," she murmured, holding him where he was.

"You haven't gotten much out of this," he murmured.

"I will."

She stroked his back and shoulders, kissed the side of his face, as she began to move her hips in a slow, provocative rhythm. Moments ago he had been on the verge of exhaustion. Incredibly, she aroused him again, and he found he was as hard as if he hadn't just been satisfied—twice. But at least he was sure he could make it last a little longer.

He turned his head and their lips met. "I want this to be good for you, too," he whispered.

"It is."

"It will be," he answered. Easing to his side, he took her with him, stroking her breasts, then down her body, finding the hot, wet center of her pleasure.

It gave him some measure of satisfaction to see her expression intensify, to hear her breathing accelerate.

This time he had enough control to wait until he felt her inner muscles contract before he let himself follow her over the edge.

They clung together, both holding on for dear life as orgasm took them.

She gasped out his name. Words were beyond him. He gave her one heartfelt kiss before easing away and flopping onto the mattress. Almost at once, his body felt like lead. He slept then, thankful for the mercy of oblivion, because he didn't know how he would ever face Gillian again, not after the way he'd acted like a wild animal in rut.

Sometime later, his eyes snapped open. It took several moments for him to remember where he was and what had happened. And when he did, a horrible sick feeling blocked his windpipe.

Chapter Thirteen

Gillian was in the bathroom getting dressed, hoping that she wouldn't disturb Alex. He looked pale and sick, and she knew from what she'd read that he needed to sleep off the rest of the drug's effects. So she was giving him as much time as she could before she had to go downstairs to work.

That was an excellent reason for staying out of his way now. But that wasn't her only motive. She knew Alexander McMullin pretty well. And she knew how he was going to react to what had happened this afternoon. He hadn't done anything wrong besides try to pose as one of her customers. But he was going to blame himself for letting Babs slip him that drugged drink. And he was going to blame himself for what had happened afterward. She wanted to tell him that it was all right. But she suspected he wouldn't listen. More than that, she suspected that any chance of a relationship between them was over, because he'd be too embarrassed to face her on any kind of personal level. In his eyes, he'd made a major mistake that had led to a humiliating episode. And she'd been there to witness that humiliation.

But she was keeping an ear out, in case he needed her

help when he woke up. And when she heard a loud curse from the other room, she came flying through the door.

He was looking around, his face gray and panicked, his breath coming too quickly.

"Alex, you're okay. You're in my room," she said as she hurried across the rug. She started to sit beside him, then thought better of invading his space.

He had pushed himself to a sitting position, but he still looked like he was freaking out, and fear leaped inside her chest. One of the worst things she knew about this damn drug was that it sometimes left its victims brain damaged. She had tried to keep herself from thinking about that. Now she knew she had to consider the possibility.

"Alex, what is it? What's wrong?" she asked anxiously.

When he answered the question with another curse, the fear grew to intolerable proportions. Unable to stop herself, she came down onto the bed and took him by the shoulders.

"What?" she asked again urgently.

He ran a shaky hand through his hair, looking sick.

"Alex, say something coherent to me," she ordered.

Because he kept his gaze averted and his lips closed, she tried another tactic. Dropping her hands away from him, she said, "I promise not to talk about the damn drug. But I have to know you're all right. So look at me and say something intelligent. Or I'll have to call the doctor."

That got his attention. His head jerked up. When he lifted his gaze and focused on her, she at least knew he'd heard and understood her. But then his gaze slid away again, as though he couldn't stand the sight of her. Probably he couldn't.

Suddenly her throat felt tight. She wanted to fold him into her arms. She wanted to tell him that there had been no dishonor in what they'd done together. She wanted him to understand that taking care of his raging needs had made her feel closer to him. But she kept all that locked inside herself, because she knew he'd simply think she was offering kind words and comfort out of sympathy.

He cleared his throat—too loudly, and she waited with her stomach in knots for what he was going to say.

As if trying out his voice, he said, "I want to get up and walk out of here. But I came on business."

"Okay," she answered, relieved that he was coherent, and that he was talking business, even if he did want to leave.

"You turned off the microphone, right?"

"Yes."

"Turn it back on."

"Okay." When she'd done as he asked, she looked at him questioningly.

"Courville isn't happy with having you here. He's pulling you off the case."

She blinked in astonishment. "Did I hear that right? He's ordering me out of here? After all I've been through."

Alex's mouth hardened. "Unfortunately, we thought we'd secured your boss's cooperation. But he's chickened out."

This time it was her turn to curse. "He can't! We don't have the information we need."

"Yeah, but he's gonna do it. Tomorrow. Which means we have to get something accomplished tonight."

He looked wildly around the room, as though he'd remembered something else. "Where the hell is my briefcase? Don't tell me it's down in the damn parlor."

"No," she assured him. "I guess you don't remember, but I brought it up here, then put it in the closet."

"Thank God."

She hurried across the room and retrieved the case. When

she turned, he was standing naked on unsteady feet, gathering up his clothing. "Give me a minute, will you."

"Okay." Stepping back into the bathroom, she fiddled with her hairdo, but her mind stayed on Alex. After a couple of minutes, she stuck her head back into the room. He was moving slowly. He'd gotten his pants on, but his shirt was still unbuttoned.

When he saw her watching, he shot her a dark look, and she averted her eyes. The next time she checked, he was fully dressed, except for his shoes, and was fumbling with the catches on the briefcase. She had to press her arms to her sides to keep from helping him.

When the top popped up, he pulled out a manila envelope and extracted a man's picture. Apparently determined to focus on business, he said, "You saw a guy with one of those teenage girls. Is this him?"

She crossed the room and took the offered photograph. "It could be. I only saw him in profile. This is a head-on shot. Sorry," she added in answer to his disappointed look. "Who is he?"

"District Attorney Primeaux."

"You think he was fooling with one of those kids?"

"He's not a very nice guy." Sounding more coherent by the minute, Alex told her what they'd learned about the D.A. Then concluded, "Nobody would talk about it on the record. But we heard he likes teenage prostitutes. That's why I brought you the photograph."

"I'd like to help," she said. "But I can't be positive."

"Well, that's not the only avenue to pursue." He looked at the wall clock. "You have to go down soon, right?"

"Yes," she answered, torn. She didn't want to leave him alone, but at the same time she knew he needed some distance from her. And she also knew that she was in big trouble if she stepped out of line again.

"Maybe we can wrap this up tonight. That was my plan." He stopped and swallowed, looking like he was going to keel over. But he kept himself erect. "Are you willing to go back to that office we were in and search more thoroughly?"

"With you?" she asked, trying to keep a note of incredulity out of her voice.

"No. That's too dangerous." He made a snorting sound. "Especially when I'm weaving around like a mongoose. But I can wire you for sound."

She ignored the first part and focused on business. "Okay."

Apparently he couldn't stay on his feet much longer, because he dropped down heavily into the chair and sat there with his eyes closed for several seconds.

He looked like he might pass out, but somehow she kept herself from rushing to him.

To her relief, he remained sitting up. After taking several breaths, he said, "This is what we're going to do. I'm going to stay in the bathroom. You spend the evening as usual. Then you can search the office."

Well, so much for distance. "I do my job…in front of you?" she exclaimed.

"Pretend I'm not here."

Yeah, sure, she thought. But at least she could keep an eye on him while her johns were sleeping. So she made the bed, then finished getting ready for work before leaving the room and going downstairs.

As soon as Gillian left, Alex heaved himself out of the chair and crossed to the bathroom. Turning on the cold water in the sink, he stuck his head under the faucet, which helped clear his brain.

Finally he raised his eyes and peered at his visage in the

mirror. He looked as though someone had dug him up out of a grave and thrown him on a slab in the morgue.

He was still feeling pretty sick and shaky, but he wasn't going to tell that to Gillian. He wasn't going to tell anyone. And he was hoping she would keep quiet about what had happened to him.

On the other hand, he did know that the two of them were going to have to talk about it. But not now. Not until he felt a lot more sure of himself.

Lord, could you become addicted to the stuff after one dose? He told himself that couldn't be true. Still, a worm of fear slithered down his spine.

With a grimace, he practiced making his voice sound normal. Then he got out the equipment that he'd stowed in the briefcase, along with the picture.

They'd sent Gillian in here without a transmitter. But since she was being pulled out tomorrow, Alex had insisted on changing the rules. The next time she did some sneaking around, she was going to use the wire he'd brought.

Meanwhile, he tested the small device by calling Rich in the van.

"Alex! Where have you been?" his partner asked immediately.

"Busy," he snapped, glad that Rich couldn't see him. "I'll tell you about it later," he added, wondering what the hell he was going to say about the couple of hours he'd lost. He'd rather say he'd been in a drunken stupor than admit the truth.

"You've got something for us?" Rich asked.

"Not yet. We're taking a break while Gillian carries out her usual duties."

"Well, I have something interesting I've been itching to tell you," Rich answered.

"Yeah?"

"Courville finally sent us a report on that body you found in the trunk." Rich waited a beat before continuing. "It's a guy named Sid Laurent."

"How did you identify him?"

"Dental records. They removed his fingerprints, but they forgot about his gold tooth."

Alex laughed.

"Get this, he works for District Attorney Primeaux."

Alex couldn't hold back a startled exclamation. "Does Primeaux know about the ID yet?"

"Not to my knowledge."

"I'd like to be there to see his reaction."

Before they could continue the conversation, he heard the bedroom door open. "Gotta go," he whispered, then switched off the transmitter.

In the room, he could hear Gillian with a man. He'd overheard this scene a lot of times. Now he couldn't stop himself from opening the door the barest crack and watching Gillian work. He couldn't help admiring her smooth handling of her customer. And he couldn't help wondering how she'd really felt about the session in that very bed with him earlier.

DOWNSTAIRS Maurice Gaspard was sitting in the elegantly furnished room where he liked to relax if he had to spend any time in the bordello.

It was nothing like the office. Instead it was a haven for a man of taste and refinement. The chairs were deep, rich leather. The carpet had come from an auction at one of the finest houses in the city.

On the side table sat a snifter of the Napoleon brandy he had told Cynthia that he kept around for special customers. Really, it was for himself. He had expensive tastes, and this operation was keeping him very well supplied. Too bad he couldn't skim off a little more of the money. But that would be too risky considering that the owner of the bordello was actually Jerome Senegal. The guy might have carved out a place for himself in the legitimate business world, but he was a very dangerous character.

Of course, Cynthia thought he, Maurice, owned this whorehouse. But it wasn't true. He was just an employee, the same as she was. Maintaining the fiction served two purposes. It kept her in line, and it kept him out of trouble with Senegal, because his boss had told him that no one was to know about the ownership.

He studied the computer records of the earnings of each girl. The new one, Gillian Stanwick, was doing very well. But he didn't trust her. And if what Babs had told him turned out to be true—then she was a dead woman.

But right now, he couldn't put off the phone call that he was supposed to make.

So he dialed the number and waited with his heart pounding for someone to pick up.

"Hello," a Cajun-accented voice said.

"Gaspard here."

"Let me get the boss."

Long seconds ticked by before Senegal came on the line. "Maurice, it's good to hear from you," he said, as though this call hadn't been arranged all along. "How are our operations going?"

"Very well. The girls have brought in more money so far this month than their take from the first two weeks of last month."

"That's good. But what I want to hear about is the drug distribution operation."

"Yes," Maurice said, and began reading numbers off the sheet of paper he'd brought along.

WHEN GILLIAN'S CUSTOMER was sleeping, she crossed to the bathroom, looking anxious. "Are you okay?" she asked as she stepped into the room and closed the door.

Maybe because he was still feeling like a car functioning on three cylinders, he snapped, "What? Did you expect to find me lying unconscious on the floor?"

"No," she answered briskly. "And if you happen to be wondering, I saw Babs downstairs."

"The bitch who slipped me the Category Five?" he asked sharply.

"Yes. I told her you were my old boyfriend, and you'd been pestering me. I told her I helped you out up here, but I made you give me all the money in your wallet in exchange for my cooperation. I told her you left by the back door and that you're probably home sleeping off the aftereffects."

"Quick thinking," he approved.

"Since we were talking, I asked her where she scored the stuff," Gillian said. "Of course she wouldn't say. I could tell she loved holding out on me."

"Damn. Guess it was too much to hope she'd finger her dealer."

"Babs sure didn't hold back on gloating about what she'd done to you, however, she sneered about how she thought about giving me a dose of the drug. Then she decided it would be more fun to give it to you."

"She told you all that?" Alex pressed, thinking the woman was a fool for talking so much.

"She was gleeful. She'd just been with a big, important client who had asked for her specifically, so she was feeling expansive. She said she figures I can't do anything about her drugging you, because I'll get in trouble with the madam if I step out of line."

"You're not going to be here long enough for that."

She nodded tightly.

"So let me tell you what I have in mind for your last night," he said, switching back to the business they still had to conduct. "Like I said, I think our best bet is for you to search that office again. I mean, do a thorough job, because it's the most likely place where you're going to find anything."

"Okay," she answered, matching his matter-of-fact tone.

"Here's the transmitter I want you to wear." He went on to show her the microphone and the other equipment. "But you can't put it on until you're finished work."

As though nothing personal had happened between them a little while ago, they talked about her search mission for another few minutes. Then she was ready to go wake up her john and tell him what a great time they'd had together. After that she and the john went back downstairs.

It was half an hour longer before Gillian returned to her room with another man. She went through the usual routine.

When she had the guy snoozing, Alex told her about Sid Laurent.

"Another connection to the D.A.," she murmured.

"Yeah. Interesting, isn't it?"

"Maybe the guy dug up some of his boss's secrets and Primeaux got rid of him." She paused. "You think he ordered the killing?"

Alex shrugged. "From what I heard about him, it's not impossible."

Again, they had to cut the conversation short because Gillian had to get back to her customer.

Alex listened to her wake-up routine, half admiring her technique and half hating her for being so good at it.

This time, when she went down, she was gone for several hours. Alex felt his chest tightening as he waited for her to return. Finally, the door opened, and she slipped back in.

"Where were you?" he demanded.

"Sometimes there are men who come here to relax—and not for sex. Some of them wanted my company, so I stayed downstairs."

He gave her a tight nod, thinking that she was probably glad to have had that duty. It was easier than taking men up here and drugging them—and easier than dealing with the half-cracked man hiding in the bathroom.

But now the evening was drawing to a close and they had to deal with each other.

"So what else am I looking for?" she asked brusquely.

"Anything that ties up the drug distribution. Or that implicates specific customers," he said.

"We searched the desk. Where else should I look?"

"Some secret hiding place that's not obvious." Reaching in his case, he took out a set of lock picks. "You might need these."

"Right," she answered, as though he was giving her loose change to use in a soda machine.

He was prepared to help her with the wire, but she knew how to attach it. Still, he insisted on checking it.

"Pull up your blouse," he said.

She did, and he touched the tape that held the transmitter. They both went very still as his finger glided over her skin.

He pulled his hand back.

"Alex."

"What?"

"Stop pretending you feel fine. And stop pretending you don't care about us…because I know you do."

His eyes narrowed. "That's a hell of a thing to say—now."

"I know. But I needed you to hear it. It's a…taste…of what I want to say later."

"Go down and search that office," he ordered.

"I intend to."

Whirling, she started for the door. He wanted to call her back and take her in his arms. He wanted to thank her for what she'd done earlier—for him. He wanted to admit that they had things to talk about. But not now. She had work to do, and thinking about him would be dangerous.

That's what he told himself. And it was true. But he was still glad of the excuse to postpone the inevitable.

THE HOUSE WAS SILENT as Gillian stepped into the back hall. She took that as a good sign. Briskly, she made her way to the office. But she'd barely gotten to the first floor when she stopped short and drew in a quick breath. She'd almost bumped into Madam Dupré, who was gliding down the darkened hall like a ghost, obviously on some urgent errand of her own.

"What?" Alex demanded in her ear.

She stayed silent until the woman was out of the way. "Madam Dupré is out and about."

"Great," Alex muttered.

"But she didn't see me. She was going the other way."

"Maybe you'd better come back for a while."

"I've come this far. I want to get it over with."

Cutting off the conversation she started for the office again, entering by way of the secret entrance Pam had shown them.

"I'm here," she told Alex.

"Good," he answered.

He had told her to look in places that weren't obvious, so she started with the baseboards, seeing if any of them were loose. She even lifted up sections of the rug to see if there were loose floorboards underneath. But there was nothing so sophisticated.

CYNTHIA STEPPED OUTSIDE the back door of the bordello and looked down the darkened alley. She hated being ordered to come out here, but she had no choice.

Gaspard had told her to give Jack Smith the bartender his weekly payoff, and she had the money in her purse.

Drugs for money.

She liked the idea of sex for money much better. She could understand appealing to the baser instincts of men. All men wanted sex. If they weren't getting it at home, then they were free to come to her house and relieve their tensions with her girls.

Drugs were another matter. Less honest. There was no basic human need for mind-altering substances. Life was mind altering enough. But she would do as she was told, as long as it kept her house in business.

Reaching into her purse, she pulled out a pack of cigarettes and tapped one out. Then she lit it and inhaled. Not deeply. Tobacco was a drug, too. A drug more dangerous than smokers imagined. She didn't allow the girls in her house to smoke. Usually she didn't indulge herself. But it made a good cover story for why she was out here in the dark.

Hating the smell of garbage from the cans near the door, she walked a little way down the alley, then tapped her foot impatiently as she waited for Jack.

GILLIAN ALMOST MISSED the secret compartment in the credenza. But when she lightly tapped on what looked like decorative carving on a front panel, it sounded hollow. So she played around with the design and a panel slid open.

"I found something," she whispered. "A secret drawer."

"That sounds promising."

Inside, she found a manila envelope and shuffled through

the contents. Her nose wrinkled as she took in the subject matter.

"It's a stack of very nasty photographs. Pictures you definitely wouldn't want to leave lying around. Naked men in bed with the women here. And I don't mean they're sleeping. These pictures are sexually explicit."

"Taken with those hidden cameras."

"I guess the camera wasn't just for fun. Madam Dupré must be using them for blackmail purposes."

"Yeah," Alex agreed.

While they talked, she browsed through the photographs, recognizing some faces she'd seen in the newspaper, on the evening news, or in the lounge.

She stopped short when she came to one particular man. Apparently, she must have made some kind of noise, because she heard Alex's voice in her ear.

"What's wrong?" he demanded. "Has somebody discovered you're in there."

"No. It's the pictures. The district attorney is definitely here. It's the same man whose picture you showed me. He's with a very young girl." She ended with a disgusted sound.

"What else?"

She turned one of the pictures over and saw a notation on the back. "Something interesting. Remember that coded book we found?"

"Yes."

"I think the same numbers and letters are on the backs of the photographs. Let me check."

"So the codes would refer to the men they have pictures of."

"Yes." I guess they couldn't risk having a plain-text version around. Not when the list is so explosive.

"Yeah. Right."

She was just opening the desk drawer when the panel

behind made a small sound, warning her that someone else was entering the room. Wishing she had a gun in her hand, she whirled to face whoever had discovered her searching the office.

Chapter Fourteen

Pam was standing in the doorway, a shocked look on her face. With her was the young girl Lily, whom Gillian had tried to help. The girl looked scared enough to wet her pants, right then and there.

"You told me we'd be safe here," she whispered.

"We are safe here, aren't we?" the other woman asked, directing the question to Gillian.

"Yes, Pam," she answered, so Alex would know who had just shown up. This was a complication that neither one of them needed, but at least it wasn't Gaspard.

"Who's with her?" Alex demanded, his voice low and urgent in her ear.

"What are you doing here, and why do you have Lily with you?" Gillian asked. After the last conversation they'd had about the young girls, Pam was the last person she would have expected to side with Lily.

"First things first," Pam shot back. "You're obviously up to something."

"So are you," Gillian answered.

Pam stepped into the room, bringing the girl with her, then shut the panel.

Thinking that she would be out of this whole situation

in a few hours, Gillian made a split-second decision. "I'm working for a government agency, getting evidence."

"Of what?"

She couldn't tell them the real reason, but the photographs on the desk gave her a good cover story. Gesturing toward them, she said, "Getting the goods on guys who frequent this place." Then, switching the subject back to Pam, she pressed, "What about you? You're not the typical slave girl around here. You're too aggressive. And you keep turning up in places where you shouldn't be."

Pam lifted one shoulder. "You've got that right."

"Are you working for the Feds?" Gillian tried.

The other woman laughed. "Hardly."

When Lily cringed, Pam sobered. "My little sister was a runaway who got hooked in by Gaspard. She smuggled a note out to me. But before I could get to her, she died." Pam kept her gaze on Gillian, and she understood that going into details in front of the girl was a bad idea. She also understood the emotions coursing through the other woman because she'd felt something very similar. "I came to get even with the bastards who run this place. I help get the underage girls out of here, when I can. And while I'm at it, I'm transferring some funds to my own account, so I'll be set up when I leave." Pam turned to Lily. "You'll stay here until the coast is clear. Then I'll get you to the back door and you can go home."

"My father will kill me," the girl mumbled.

"Who is your father?" Gillian asked, thinking that when she got out of this house, she was going to make it her personal business to arrest the guy for negligence.

"It's not his fault," Lily protested.

"Just give me his name, so I can make sure you get home," Gillian tried.

"Tanner Harrison," the girl whispered.

Gillian's exclamation was echoed by Alex's curse. Neither Pam nor Lily heard him, though, because it came directly to her ear through the receiver she was wearing. Tanner Harrison was one of the other New Orleans Confidential agents. She knew he'd been out of town on an assignment.

Lily tipped her head to one side and studied Gillian. "You look shocked. Like you know him," she murmured.

"I don't know him. But I've heard of him. He works for a government agency, doesn't he?" she asked, falling back on the generic term she'd used earlier.

"Yes."

"How did he let this happen?" she asked in a tight voice.

The girl quickly jumped to her father's defense. "It wasn't his fault. I was living with my mom. In London. My stepfather..." Her voice trailed off, then she started again. "I couldn't stay there with him in the house. So I came here looking for Dad. But he was out of town. Then I ran out of money..."

"I'll get you to your dad," Gillian promised.

In her ear, Alex was speaking. "I've got to tell Stewart about this. I'll be back as soon as I can. Get the girl to the front door, and Rich will drive up with the van."

She couldn't acknowledge his statement or his order, not without giving away that he was eavesdropping on the conversation. Could she trust Pam? She didn't know for sure. But so far the woman had helped her out. So she said, "You stay here with Lily. Let me make sure the coast is clear. Then I'll have a friend meet her at the front door."

"Who?"

"His name is Rich. He's someone I work with."

She debated leaving the packet of pictures, then decided she'd better take them with her. Scooping them up, she slipped them into the waistband of her slacks, then she turned toward the door.

"Wait right here, and I'll get Rich," she said, then exited the room. After taking a few steps away from the door, she breathed out a little sigh.

MAURICE GASPARD was on his way down the hall toward the office. There was something about the conversation with his boss that had disturbed him.

He couldn't put his finger on what it was. But he knew that he was working for a ruthless man and that he had to protect himself. Like it might be useful to have some of those blackmail photos in his possession. And some of the cash that was kept in the office.

He was about to turn the corner when he heard the office door open.

Thrusting only his head forward, he saw Gillian Stanwick step into the hall and say, "Wait right here."

He didn't catch all of the last part, but it had something to do with a man named Rich.

Who the hell was Rich? That boyfriend of hers that Babs had told him about? He'd wondered if the whore was lying because she was jealous of Gillian's new importance in the house, but now he didn't know.

He had never been happy about Cynthia's hiring the woman. He could go after her now. But it was more important to get the man—who was certainly in the room.

So he waited for her to disappear, then pulled the gun he kept tucked in a shoulder holster under his arm and rushed toward the office.

"Freeze," he shouted as he opened the door. Then he blinked. It wasn't a man in the room. It was two girls—Pam and Lily.

Before he had time to rearrange his thinking, something

flew through the air, hitting him in the face. When it covered his head and shoulders, he realized it was a comforter.

"Run," Pam shouted.

While he was still pulling the damn thing off, he heard their pounding feet.

"Go," PAM ORDERED, pushing Lily toward the back of the house. "The other way. He's between you and the front door. You have to get out the back, while you can."

The girl gave her a terrified look, then started for the kitchen and into the back hall. Pulling open the door, she stepped into the alley. But a flash of movement stopped her. Someone was coming.

She was trapped. She couldn't go back and she couldn't go forward.

Her only option was to duck behind a smelly garbage can, where she waited with her heart pounding.

"You're late," a voice said in the darkness, and she recognized Madam Dupré, the old bitch who ran the house.

Peeking around the trash can, she saw the woman and a man whose white shirt stood out in the light from overhead.

"I can't just walk away from my job," he said. "I have to wait until there's a break in the action."

"The point is, Jack, do you have the merchandise?" the madam said.

"Yes. And you have the money, right?"

"As always. Let's get this over with. I want to go back inside."

The two figures moved closer together.

In the next second, a man wearing a mask stepped around the corner. A gun in his hand glinted in the light from the overhead bulb. Both the madam and the man named Jack looked up.

"What..." Jack had time to say before Lily heard two

spitting noises. From the movies she'd seen, she guessed she was hearing bullets from a silencer.

Jack and the madam both fell to the cement.

Lily couldn't hold back a gasp.

The man with the gun whirled toward her, taking in the inconvenient fact that he wasn't alone. In that split second, she was already running for her life. Something whizzed by her head, but she didn't look back, silently praying that she could get away. And when she reached the crowds on Bourbon Street, she knew she'd made more than one miraculous escape that evening.

GILLIAN WAS STANDING by the front door, looking for the van. It hadn't come yet. What the heck was holding Rich up? Hadn't he gotten the message? Or had he parked a couple of blocks away and gotten caught in traffic?

She heard footsteps and thought it might be Alex coming down to supervise. He was still shaky and needed to stay out of sight. She could handle this on her own. She whirled, an annoyed comment on her lips. It died before she could speak.

It wasn't Alex in the hallway behind her.

Instead she was facing Maurice Gaspard, and he was holding a weapon.

Suddenly she was sorry she was on her own.

Even in the darkened hallway, she could see his expression was fierce. "I knew Cynthia never should have hired you, you sneaky little bitch. What the hell is going on?" he growled, leveling the gun at her middle, where she knew it would do a great deal of damage. A belly shot led to a slow, painful death.

Through her dry lips, she answered, "Nothing."

"Don't tell me 'nothing.' You and the other two girls were in the office. What were you doing there?"

"I didn't know it was the office. We like to go there to unwind."

He laughed, a sound like fingernails on tin. "What were you really doing, *chère?* Looking for money? Or is that where you take your boyfriend?"

"What boyfriend?"

"The one Babs told me about. You think she believes that you're finished with him?" he asked, punctuating the question with a jerk of the gun.

Behind him, she saw a flicker of movement and she knew it was Alex creeping down the hall.

Realizing they had an opportunity to get a confession on tape, she said, "Babs is a liar. And a cheat. Do you know she got a hold of some Category Five and gave it away?" she asked.

"That's a lie. The Category Five is locked up," he said, then scowled. "How do you know about that?"

"Everybody knows about it," she tossed out, lying through her teeth. "Have you tried it? Does it make you hot?"

"I don't take that drug!"

Gillian moved her shoulders in a sexy shrug. "Well, that doesn't matter. I don't have any boyfriend. Actually, you're the one who fascinates us. Pam and I go into the office to talk about you. About how much we'd like to make love with you. Why didn't you ever come up to my room the way you promised?"

He gave her an assessing look. "I've been busy, but maybe you should spread your legs for me tonight."

She struggled not to react to the crude suggestion or the tone of his voice, but his smile told her he knew how it had made her feel.

"And after that, I'll turn you over to Tony the Knife. He

likes to carve people up, *chère.* You should have seen what he did to the last poor bastard he worked on. Sid Laurent.''

Behind Gaspard, Gillian saw Alex stiffen.

''What did Laurent do to you?'' she asked.

''Not to me. To the people I work for. He was in charge of the initial distribution of the drug. And he calculated the dosage wrong. Men were getting too much and getting sick. He paid for the mistake. Just like you'll pay for your snooping around here.''

She was confused. She'd thought Laurent worked for the D.A. He worked for the drug dealers, too? She didn't have time to ponder that.

Alex had started moving soundlessly down the hall again. He was almost on top of Gaspard, his arms raised.

Then one of the old floorboards made a small creaking sound and Gaspard was momentarily distracted. She used that split second to kick out at his leg—throwing him off balance—just before Alex brought his fists down on the man's head.

He gasped and fell, the weapon discharging as he went down, but the bullet went into the wall.

Upstairs women began to scream, and they heard running footsteps in the upper hall.

''Stay up there, if you don't want to get shot,'' Alex shouted, then grabbed Gillian's arm, guiding her toward the back of the building.

The door was ajar and they fled into the night.

But they had taken only a few steps when a grisly sight greeted them. Jack and Madam Dupré lay on the ground, both bleeding from chest wounds.

Kneeling down, they each checked one of the victims. Gillian found that the madam was dead.

But as Alex bent over Jack, he shouted, ''He's still alive. Call an ambulance.''

The man's eyes fluttered open. "Too…late," he whispered.

Gillian knew it was true. She knelt beside Alex who was saying, "Tell me who did this to you."

Jack tried to focus on him. "What…you…doing… here?" he whispered.

"I'm on this case." Alex spoke rapidly. "I was undercover in the bar. If you tell me what happened, I'll get the bastards who did this to you. There's no sense in your protecting anyone now."

A trickle of blood oozed from Jack's mouth as he tried to speak. "The Cajun…mob…"

He stopped speaking again and Gillian thought they had lost him. But his lips moved again. "The head kingpin is Jerome Senegal. And the mob's not working alone. They…have a partner. His name is…"

He never finished the last word. But in his dying moments he had given them the lead they needed to plan their next move in shutting down the drug network.

Sirens blared in the distance. Suddenly the alley was lit with the flashing lights of police cars.

Rich came running down the alley. "I got jammed up on a one-way street. When I got to the front door, nobody was there. Where's Harrison's daughter?" he demanded.

Gillian shook her head. "Gaspard found her and Pam in the office. I hope she got away."

"I hope she has sense to go back home," Alex said.

Uniformed officers poured into the house, rounding up the girls who were in various states of undress. Babs gave Gillian a dangerous look as she was herded off with the others in a paddy wagon.

But the girls were the only catch of the night. Gaspard had disappeared. And Pam was nowhere to be found. Apparently she'd gotten away, too. Or perhaps she was hiding in some secret passageway in the house. And she would emerge when it was safe.

Good for her, Gillian thought.

Before the department had hustled her away for debriefing, she'd been able to get one important message to Alex.

"I won't put anything in my report about Babs giving you the drug," she'd said.

"I appreciate that," he'd answered, his voice tight.

In the next moment, Lieutenant LeBarron led her off to a debriefing room. And Conrad Burke, head of New Orleans Confidential came in to take charge of Alex.

AFTER ENDLESS HOURS of answering questions and filling out forms, Gillian was finally free to leave.

She knew Alex had gone off to the Department of Public Safety, and she suspected that she wasn't going to see him again any time soon.

But as she stepped out the staff entrance, a car pulled up beside her and the door swung open.

When she saw Alex was behind the wheel, her jaw dropped open.

"Get in," he said tersely.

She might have refused. Instead she slid into the passenger seat, then looked at him questioningly. "Where are we going?"

"Not far."

He didn't speak again, and she sat beside him with her nerves screaming, casting furtive glances at the tense set of his jaw. She'd told him they had things to talk about. Now she was afraid to hear whatever he had to say.

He drove to a house she had never seen not far from the French Quarter, unlocked the gate to the moonlit courtyard and led her inside. It was so strange to see the moon again, after she'd been inside for weeks.

"Where are we?" she asked as the gate closed behind them.

"My place."

She looked around at the unfamiliar surroundings, listened to the sound of a fountain gurgling somewhere nearby. "You didn't live here the last time..." Her voice trailed off.

"Not long after we broke up, a friend steered me to a sweetheart of a foreclosure sale. I've been fixing the place up ever since."

"Oh." When he made no move to go inside, she looked around at the neatly tended flower beds, then spotted the lion's head fountain attached to one wall.

"It's easier to talk out here—in the dark," he said. "Why don't you sit down?"

Wondering what he wanted to say, she dropped into a vintage metal lawn chair and looked at him inquiringly.

He paced the length of the patio, turned around and came partway back, running a hand through his hair before he cleared his throat. "My parents weren't married when I was born. They got hitched, but it didn't last. They divorced—then each found different mates.

"My mom and dad have both been married five times. His shortest marriage was four months. I've got so many stepsisters and brothers that it's hard to keep up with them. Half brothers and sisters. And kids who might be the son or daughter of someone Mom or Dad married. Sometimes, I think I'm related or semirelated to half the city's population."

He had never revealed any of that. She could only stare at him as he made a snorting sound and continued.

"I shuffled around a lot from one house to the other. So I never had a feeling of stability. A lot of times, I felt like I was the last one in line for attention."

"Why are you telling me?" she asked, unable to keep her voice steady.

"Because I come from a background where I've seen more marriages that go to hell than work out. And I know what it does to a kid who grows up being shuffled around from family to family and ignored or worse most of the time. I swore I'd never do that to a kid of my own. I swore that I'd never give myself the chance to do it."

He fell silent, and she tried to interpret what he had been telling her.

"What are you saying exactly?" she asked. "Are you explaining to me why you're going to walk out of my life again?"

He answered with a low curse. "No! That's not why I brought you here. To my home. My refuge, if that's what you want to call it."

"Then what?"

"I'm trying to make you understand why a boy who grew up being carted from pillar to post might think he'd make a mess of any marriage he got into. I'm trying to give you some insight into why I walked out on the most satisfying relationship I ever had. I know we had something good, but I was afraid to trust it."

The large lump that had formed in her windpipe made it hard to swallow or speak. But she managed to say, "And now?"

Again he ran a hand through his hair. "Now I'm asking you to take me back."

She wanted to shoot out of the chair and wrap her arms around him. But she stayed where she was, because she still wasn't sure that embracing him was the right thing to do. "Why?"

"Because I love you," he said in a strangled voice.

"Did I hear that right?" she asked.

"I hope so. I said I love you. It's hard to say. After the way I turned into a basket case this afternoon."

"Oh, Alex." Unable to hold back, she surged out of the chair then and into his arms, clinging to him for dear life. "This afternoon gave me a chance to do something for you. And I got something out of it, too."

"I hope so."

"One afternoon with you under the influence of Category Five doesn't change anything."

He was listening intently, so she decided to go for broke. "The real issue is that you hurt me—so much—when you walked away from us."

To her astonishment, he nodded in agreement. "I know. Back then I told myself it was for the best. It was better to cut you off clean, than open us both up to a lifetime hurt. Now I know I was protecting myself. I wanted—needed—you in my life, but I was afraid to trust the feelings." He stopped and gulped. "Still, you were right, I kept tabs on you. I knew what you were doing. I knew you'd entered the police academy. I even found out your grades. You were right up there at the top of your class, and I was so proud of you."

She might have resented that, but she understood his motives now.

"I know I broke your heart two years ago," he whispered. "I hope I get a chance to mend it. I hope we've already started that process."

She felt tears film her eyes. "Why didn't you say something?"

"Where? When? You were living in a whorehouse. It didn't exactly seem like the right setting. Then, this afternoon, you saw me at my absolute worst."

"That wasn't *your* worst. That was Category Five," she reassured him again.

"Whatever. It made me feel like a jerk. I thought I could never face you again. But then I knew I had to, if I was going to get what I want."

"Which is?"

"You. For my wife."

"Your wife!" she exclaimed.

"I—I can't promise I'll ever be ready for a family. I think I have to work up to the concept."

"Oh, Alex, I've been in love with you all this time. And I thought I'd never get close to you again. We'll work it out together. I'll show you how warm and giving a relationship can be. And when you meet my parents, you'll understand the good foundation they gave me. I hope my family can give you all the stability you missed growing up. We never had a lot of money. But we always had a lot of love."

He hugged her more tightly. "I want to meet them. But not now. Now I've got to make love to you. Only this time, I'll be in my right mind, and I can do it properly."

She wanted that, too, and started to let him lead her inside—then stopped. "I don't want to mess things up right at the beginning, but there's something else we need to talk about," she said in a hesitant voice.

"What?" he asked, suddenly guarded, and she realized he was afraid to take happiness for granted. But she had to find out something important before they went any further.

"My job. You did your best to intimidate me—to get me to drop the undercover assignment. Are you going to do that again?"

"I have to be honest. I thought LeBarron gave you a pretty tough gig—for a rookie cop."

"Yes. But I handled it."

"I know. More than handled it. You were brilliant. I

didn't think even an experienced policewoman could pull it off—but you did it.''

"Thank you for telling me that.''

"Well, it was another thing I couldn't mention until you were out of the situation. I didn't want you to start relaxing. I knew that each day in there was going to bring its own challenges.''

She nodded, knowing that he had played it the right way—after that ridiculous training session.

"Can we stop talking now and start getting physical?'' he asked, his hands stroking up and down her back as he bent his head to nuzzle her ear. When he began to worry her earlobe with his teeth, she forgot momentarily what they'd been talking about.

"Come in and see my house. I think I was fixing it up for you.''

"You're kidding!''

"Well, I couldn't admit that to myself. But I haven't brought any other women here. Only you.''

"Oh, Alex,'' she breathed, clasping his hand as he led her into the house.

When she stopped again, he looked at her questioningly. "One more thing. When we go see my parents, don't tell them the details of my assignment. Okay?''

"Are you handing me blackmail material?''

"It sounds like it.''

"Okay, we have a deal.''

He clasped her hand and led her through the darkened living room, into his bedroom and into the new life they would make together.

Epilogue

It was three days after the meltdown at the McDonough Club that Conrad Burke convened a meeting of the New Orleans Confidential agents to discuss the ongoing drug investigation.

Alex made a point of being on time because the other agents all knew that Gillian had moved in with him, and he wanted to prove that he was wide-awake and ready for work—even if he had been up half the night making love with her.

"I've got good news and bad news," Conrad said when they were all assembled in the conference room. His face took on a grieving look. "The bad news first. Wiley Longbottom is in a coma. His family has arrived in New Orleans to be with him."

There were murmurs of anger and sympathy around the table.

"It looks bad. But the doctors haven't given up on him," Conrad continued.

There was more bad news, of course. Lily Harrison hadn't surfaced. But nobody was tactless enough to mention that in front of her father who sat grim-faced a few seats down the table from Alex.

Conrad was speaking again. "And when Wiley wakes up, I want to be able to tell him that we've stopped the distribution of Category Five in New Orleans. We've already made significant progress," he went on.

"Up until now, Jerome Senegal has been able to operate as a legitimate businessman. But we finally have proof that links him to the Cajun mob—which has been actively controlling local businesses, banks, insurance companies, and the like."

"But we shut down his drug distribution center at the McDonough Club," Rich put in.

Conrad nodded. "Yes, thanks to you, Alex McMullin, and Gillian Seymour, who pulled off a very difficult undercover operation."

All eyes turned to Alex, who couldn't help flushing. "It was Gillian who had the difficult role to play," he said. "I'm very proud of her."

Rich caught his eye and gave a flicker of a smile. They both knew that Alex had lived on a knife edge of tension during the whole operation. He'd been deathly afraid that something bad would happen to her. But it had worked out all right.

"We're still looking for Maurice Gaspard, the chief pimp, of course," Conrad went on. "But when he surfaces, we'll catch him. In a related matter, police are looking for a gunman who killed the madam and the bartender. It was most likely a mob-related hit to cover their tracks because operations were failing at the McDonough Club. Meanwhile, I want to attack the mob from a different angle—and bring them down once and for all."

He looked at Seth Lewis, who was seated across the table from Alex.

"Seth is going to be the key player in this operation.

He's going to be posing as a fantastically rich businessman. And his assignment will be to seduce a megarich mob widow named Adrienne DeBlanc, who could be instrumental in cracking this case.''

There was laughter around the table, and Alex was glad that the center of the investigation had shifted away from himself.

''Sounds like a hard job, playing a rich man and playing with a rich widow,'' Mason said, the dumb comment about par for the course with him.

Seth shifted in his seat. ''Harder than you think, for a guy who grew up in the Ninth Ward,'' he said, naming one of the poorer sections of New Orleans.

''Enjoy it while you can,'' Rich advised. ''And be careful. It sounds like a plush assignment, but playing footsie with the mob is no joke. Guys who cross them end up like Sid Laurent.''

They had also dug into Laurent's background and found the mob had planted him in the D.A.'s office.

''I know the dangers,'' Seth said, bringing Alex's mind back to the new phase of the operation.

He was thinking it couldn't really be true. Nobody ever really understood the danger of an undercover assignment, until they were in the thick of it.

Gillian had admitted that to him. Admitted how much she'd counted on his being in the van watching over her while she was working at the McDonough Club. He'd felt the same way. He'd needed to guard her. But more than that, when it had come to the crunch, she'd been there for him.

He was lucky to have her with him now—for the rest of his life, he vowed.

He looked around the table at the members of the New

Orleans Confidential. When he'd come to work here, he'd envied Conrad his wife and family. Now he thought about the other single men, hoping each of them would end up as happy as he was.

*   *   *   *   *

And the story continues…
Next month don't miss the next riveting
installment of
NEW ORLEANS CONFIDENTIAL!
BULLETPROOF BILLIONAIRE
by Mallory Kane
promises to leave you breathless.

Turn the page for a sneak peek…

Chapter One

Thank God for the sisters.

Seth Lewis sent a silent prayer heavenward as he pulled up in front of the fancy wrought-iron gate of the three-story house in the Garden District of New Orleans. The hot mid-July evening and the recent rain lent a freshly painted look to everything, even the manicured lawn. Damn, he hated this part of the city and the people who lived here. He'd promised himself a long time ago that he'd never set foot in this part of town again. But this wasn't his party. He was on assignment.

He glanced at his reflection in the rearview mirror of the new Mercedes Cabriolet convertible that was part of his cover persona. He still wasn't used to the face that stared back at him. Clean-shaven. Expensive haircut. Designer suit. He lifted his chin and cocked a brow.

Seth Lewis, billionaire businessman. His lip curled in a wry grin. More like Seth Lewis, master pretender.

It was only because of his three younger sisters that he had any chance of pulling off this assignment. When he'd told them he needed to impersonate a suave continental financier, no questions asked, they'd rallied around him. Just like they had seven months ago when he'd been shipped back to the States by the Army with both his knee-cap and his dreams shattered.

They'd laughed. They'd teased. They'd pestered him with questions he refused to answer, except to assure them that it was all legal. But they'd rallied.

Mignon had forced him into her upscale Warehouse District salon and given him a complete makeover. It had been humiliating but necessary, he supposed. After all, he couldn't enter the chic multi million dollar mansion of one of the wealthiest widows in New Orleans with shaggy hair, a ratty beard and rough, broken nails. He'd drawn the line at a full body wax and a spa treatment though. A man had to hold on to some pride.

Mignon had worked miracles, just like her ad campaign promised. He'd walked in looking like a homeless man and walked out looking like a *GQ* model. No one would know he was the same person.

Serena, the elder of the twins, had taken him shopping for a designer wardrobe that probably cost more than his VA disability pension for a year, using an untraceable credit card issued by Conrad Burke, the head of New Orleans Confidential.

Teresa, the younger twin who planned to marry a millionaire as soon as she found one who fit her high standards, had decided what kind of car he should drive and had rented and furnished him a trendy apartment in the renovated Warehouse District. The lavish apartment would be his home for the duration of his "visit" to the States.

A limousine pulled up behind him and Seth recognized New Orleans District Attorney Sebastion Primeaux arriving with the mayor. He'd known he'd be in exalted company at this shindig. But the D.A. and the mayor? His target, the woman who was hosting this charity auction, sure traveled in important circles.

As Seth stepped onto the sidewalk, he assessed the other vehicles parked along First Street. Teresa had been right. Nobody drove economy iron. Every vehicle here cost at least six figures.

Seth closed his eyes for an instant, getting into character for the part he was about to play.

He was no longer a Special Forces Weapons Sergeant. His career had ended when his knee had been in the right position to save two young Iraqi kids from a bloody death. Nor was he the bored, pissed-off-at-the-world drifter who'd moped around the French quarter for several months. Not since he'd accidentally happened upon a bank robbery and neatly disarmed the idiot waving a semiautomatic weapon. His fast action and his faster field-stripping of the weapon on the spot had ended up on the evening news and had caught the attention of a Southern gentleman with a whiskey-smooth drawl and the unyielding strength of steel.

Conrad Burke had contacted Seth and invited him into an abandoned warehouse that turned out to be a high-tech operations center the like of which Seth had never seen, even in the Army.

There Burke had introduced Seth to the Confidential agency. At first Seth had laughed at the idea of a secret agency operating above the law under the auspices of the Department of Public Safety. It sounded like something out of a spy movie, but he soon discovered that Burke was deadly serious. He'd given Seth a brief rundown of the history of the agency and the reason this branch had been established in New Orleans.

Seth had listened, fascinated and bewildered. The idea that Conrad Burke had chosen him to join New Orleans Confidential because he'd been in the right place at the right time and foiled a bank robbery was daunting.

For the first time since he'd come home, Seth found himself interested in something besides his own rotten luck. Listening to Burke, he'd begun to believe he might be able to do some good. Be somebody. Make a difference.

So he'd stepped into the persona Burke had outlined for him. He told himself it would be like a special operation and he treated it that way—studying, preparing himself mentally and physically. He forgot about Seth Lewis, street kid. He was wealthy, continental, suave and filthy rich.

This assignment was nothing like a desert campaign. Even so, he felt as though he was on foreign soil. He'd grown up in the Ninth Ward, a poor, beaten-down section of the city. Now he was in the exclusive section of New Orleans that ran along St. Charles Street. His assignment, to win the confidence of the lovely widow of rumored Cajun mob mouthpiece Marc DeBlanc, then seduce her for any information she might have.

Refusing to imagine what this Garden District rich bitch who casually threw hundred-thousand-dollar parties without blinking an eye might look like, Seth squared his Gaultier-clad shoulders and prepared to beard the lioness in her den.

He hesitated with his hand on the ornate knocker, his confidence challenged by a twinge of doubt. It worried him that he was so anxious to live up to Burke's expectations. What if he failed? All he knew was that he was tired of waking up every day wondering what the hell he was going to do with his life. Burke's offer was a second chance. He was not going to blow it.

He affected a polite, bored expression as the door swung wide, releasing muted conversations, an undertone of New Orleans jazz, and soft lighting, along with a whoosh of air-conditioning.

When his eyes lit on the vision who'd opened the door

he had to clamp his jaw to keep his mouth from dropping open.

Framed in the doorway was an angel. He blinked. Working hard to maintain his cool, he remembered what Mignon had told him about the patrons of her exclusive spa salon. *The very rich are never in a hurry. They don't have to be.* So he stood there as if he had all the time in the world and let his gaze roam over the woman.

She was golden-white all over. From her sleek, pale hair pulled back from her face into some kind of intricate knot, to her simple floor-length dress, which looked like a fairy sprinkled with gold dust.

Seth took the hand she proffered, and could have sworn he saw a spark as his fingers touched her silky-smooth skin. He knew he felt it.

When he met her gaze, his heart thudded to somewhere south of his stomach. Her eyes were a deep sapphire blue. But it was the look in them that hit him like a blow. She looked sad and surprised and fearful all at once. He had an unfamiliar urge to gather her close and protect her from everything bad in the world.

"Hi," she said, her mouth turning up in a smile that stole a bit of the sadness from her eyes and lit them with delightful flickers of lighter blue. "Do come in. I'm Adrienne DeBlanc. I don't believe we've met."

Calling on his military control to keep his gaze bland and bored, Seth swallowed his surprise. This was the mob widow, answering her own door? She didn't look at all like he'd imagined....

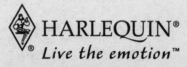

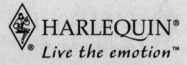

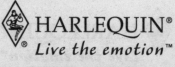

HARLEQUIN *Super*ROMANCE®

Single
FATHER

He's a man on his own, trying to raise his children.
Sometimes he gets things right. Sometimes he needs a little help....

Unfinished Business
by Inglath Cooper
(Superromance #1214) On-sale July 2004

Culley Rutherford is doing the best he can raising his young
daughter on his own. One night while on a medical conference in
New York City, Culley runs into his old friend Addy Taylor. After a
passionate night together, they go their separate ways, so Culley
is surprised to see Addy back in Harper's Mill. Now that she's
there, though, he's determined to show Addy that the three of
them can be a family.

Daddy's Little Matchmaker
by Roz Denny Fox
(Superromance #1220) On-sale August 2004

Alan Ridge is a widower and the father of nine-year-old Louemma,
who suffers from paralysis caused by the accident that killed her
mother. Laurel Ashline is a weaver who's come to the town of
Ridge City, Kentucky, to explore her family's history—a history
that includes a long-ago feud with the wealthy Ridges. Louemma
brings Alan and Laurel together, despite everything that keeps
them apart....

Available wherever Harlequin books are sold.

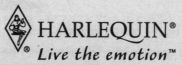

HARLEQUIN®
Live the emotion™

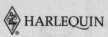

INTRIGUE

COMING NEXT MONTH

#789 BULLETPROOF BILLIONAIRE by Mallory Kane
New Orleans Confidential

New Orleans Confidential agent Seth Lewis took on the alias of a suave international tycoon to infiltrate the Cajun Mob. He'd set out to gain entry by charming the rich widow Adrienne DeBlanc into telling him everything. It wasn't long before his protective instincts surfaced for the fragile beauty, but could he risk a high-stakes case for love?

#790 MIDNIGHT DISCLOSURES by Rita Herron
Nighthawk Island

In one tragic moment, radio psychologist Dr. Claire Kos had lost everything. She survived, only to become a serial killer's next target. Blind and vulnerable to attack, she turned to FBI agent Mark Steele—the man she'd loved and lost. As the killer took aim, Mark was poised to protect the woman he couldn't live without.

#791 ON THE LIST by Patricia Rosemoor
Club Undercover

Someone wanted to silence agent Renata Fox for good. She knew the Feds had accused the wrong person of being the Chicago sniper, but her speculations had somehow landed her on the real killer's hit list. So when Gabriel Connor showed up claiming he was on the assassin's trail, Renata knew she had to put her life—and her heart—in Gabe's hands....

#792 A DANGEROUS INHERITANCE by Leona Karr
Eclipse

When a storm delivered heiress Stacy Ashford into the iron-hard embrace of Josh Spencer, it seemed their meeting was fated. Gaining her inheritance depended on reopening the eerie hotel where Josh's kid sister died. And even though Stacy's inheritance bound them to an ever-tightening coil of danger, would Josh's oath to avenge his sister cost him the one woman who truly mattered?

#793 INTENSIVE CARE by Jessica Andersen

When Dr. Ripley Davis saw another of her patients flatline, she knew someone was killing the people in her care. But before she could find the real murderer, overbearing, impossibly sexy police officer Zachary Cage accused her of the crime. It wasn't long before her fiery resolve convinced him she wasn't the prime suspect...she was the prime *target*.

#794 SUDDEN ALLIANCE by Jackie Manning

When undercover operative Liam O'Shea found Sarah Regis on the side of the road, battered and incoherent, his razor-sharp instincts warned him she was in danger. As an amnesic murder witness, her only hope for survival was to stay in close proximity to Liam. Would their sudden alliance survive the secrets she'd kept locked inside?

HICNM0704